Blueberries and Coal
& Inside the Triangle

by JD Grant

Copyright © 2013 by JD Grant
First Edition – October 2013

ISBN
978-1-4602-2391-8 (Paperback)
978-1-4602-2392-5 (eBook)

All rights reserved.

No part of this publication may be reproduced in any form, or by any means, electronic or mechanical, including photocopying, recording, or any information browsing, storage, or retrieval system, without permission in writing from the publisher.

Cover artwork by: Shasta Grant
www.sgimagines.wordpress.com
sgimagines@gmail.com

Produced by:

FriesenPress
Suite 300 – 852 Fort Street
Victoria, BC, Canada V8W 1H8

www.friesenpress.com

Distributed to the trade by The Ingram Book Company

Table of Contents

Book One - Blueberries and Coal
pages 1 – 95

Book Two - Inside the Triangle
pages 97 – 175

Blueberries and Coal

One

The usually deserted hills were crowded. Rescue vehicles, backhoes, trucks, ventilation equipment, and crowds of people were flattening the scraggly grass and brush. Anxious voices and big machinery were together producing a deafening clamor.

A cameraman scanned the scene, framing his close-up of an ominous crater before focusing again on the young TV reporter struggling to fill airtime. This drama was unfolding much too slowly.

"Coal Town—a community created by the mining industry to house and support its work force ... could be anywhere ... but this Coal Town is in northern Nova Scotia, on the island of Cape Breton ... in a shrinking place, with a dying way of life ... ."

Phonse Johnson noticed the cameraman rolling his eyes but gamely forged on with his dry monologue.

"In the early 1900s, this area was booming, with eleven active coal mines providing jobs and a healthy economy. About half the families living in that boomtown of 30,000 people depended on employment in the mines or in coal mining-related industry. People worked hard; they were strong, proud, and honest …."

The cameraman, a seasoned veteran, was shaking his head. Phonse nervously quickened his pace.

"With the worldwide shift from coal to other energy sources, the mines gradually closed. This year, the last mine in Coal Town stopped production, and unemployment has now risen above thirty percent. People have become the region's biggest export, leaving in search of work. The old coal pits are now abandoned, a legacy to a different time, a different era …."

The cameraman's smirk finally silenced the rattled reporter. Phonse glanced over to the pit area, desperately hoping for a new development, but the steady drone of the diggers continued. The cameraman panned the area again, taking focus momentarily off the nervous rookie.

"Side industries grew and fell in accordance with the fortune of the mines. Whenever layoffs or closures of pits occurred in the community, "bootleg" mines opened, providing a cheap source of heat and income supplements. These illegal, mostly surface mines pockmark various hills and fields surrounding Coal Town. When used up, or when the demand fell, they were generally filled in, gradually becoming overgrown with grass and bushes."

As the camera again turned toward him, Phonse nervously straightened his tie and babbled on earnestly.

"This is Fox Farm, apparently named for a failed business venture to raise fox pelts in the early 1900s."

The cameraman winced. Phonse began to panic, his eyes searching the area for anything reportable.

"The land is barren, with rolling grassy hills and sparse trees. Jagged stones dot the hillsides and blueberry bushes thrive in the rocky soil, filling in the sunken areas, concealing these old coal pits."

Snorting in disgust, the cameraman mimed the wrap-up sign. Deflated, Phonse complied.

"This is Phonse Johnson, CBN TV, reporting from Coal Town, Nova Scotia, where three children ...."

The camera was off.

"Dear God," she prayed fervently, "please let them be found."

Rose wasn't a religious woman. Truth be told, she'd only seen the inside of a church three, maybe four times in the past two years. But her kids .... Kneeling in the clearing overlooking the cave-in, she choked back tears, trying to remember prayers as she rocked back and forth.

These past hours had been a nightmare, filled with constant panic, frantic phone calls, bouts of weeping, and no sleep. At thirty-eight, she felt like an old woman, wrapped in her shawl, watching, waiting, and horribly, horribly alone. Her husband was in Alberta and her children ....

"Please, God, let them be okay," she sobbed, emotion wracking her frame.

Beside her on a patch of grass, her next-door neighbor, Sadie Hines, reached over to console her, gently rocking Rose in her arms. "They'll be all right, Rosie," she crooned, "They'll be all right."

"Oh, Sadie," Rose shuddered, "I'll never forgive myself."

"Sshh, Rosie," assured her neighbor, "They'll be fine, just you wait."

"Mrs. MacDonald?" a male voice queried from behind the two ladies.

"Yes?" said Rose, turning hopefully.

"I'm Phonse Johnson, a reporter with CBN television," the rookie replied, peering through wire-rimmed glasses. "We're covering the cave-in, and would like to hear more about your kids. I realize you're going through a lot right now, but everyone should know about the dangers of these old pits. Can you help us?"

Rose knew the media would publicize this event with or without her approval. Three children trapped in a mine was news! She'd rather the real story be told than an invented one.

Sadie mistook her moment of thoughtfulness for hesitation. "Can't you people leave this woman alone? She's got more to worry about than giving you a story!"

"Wait, Sadie," cautioned Rose, touching her friend's hand. "I don't mind. Look around; everyone is trying to help." She nodded at the reporter, "I'll speak with you, but I want to know your questions first."

Smiling gratefully, Phonse sat beside Rose, quickly scrawling a proposed script.

"Don't worry, Mrs. MacDonald, no surprises," the spectacled reporter assured, motioning for the cameraman to join them. While Rose looked over his notes, Phonse retrieved an empty red wagon, placing it back nearer the pit opening and machine activity. The cameraman motioned and the camera was once again rolling.

"This is Coal Town, Nova Scotia. Half the town is here at Fox Farm hills, anxiously awaiting word of Rose MacDonald's children. Miners and rescue workers have been working round-the-clock to open an old bootleg coal pit where the children are believed trapped."

Gesturing at the activity behind them, Phonse asked, "Mrs. MacDonald, could you tell us a bit about your family, and how all this came about?"

Rose cleared her throat, trying to ignore the camera pointed in her direction. She wasn't used to public speaking and had never been on television before. "I have three children," she began, "Karen, fifteen, Bobby, eleven, and Tommy, seven …."

Two

"Tommy! Tommy! Get out of there!" yelled Karen. "Those old pits aren't safe! They could cave in or collapse around you—and then you'd know it." She punctuated her statement with a definitive nod.

The wiry young boy looked up at his teenage sister and slowly crawled out of the modestly deep concave depression in the side of the hill. His face was smudged with dirt, disguising his many freckles, and his hair, as usual, stuck out in all directions.

"Karen," he complained, "stop buggin' me. There's tons of berries down here and they're big ones."

"How come you two are always arguin'?" questioned Bobby, almost twelve. "Let's get these berries picked, so Ma can make some muffins and pies tonight."

"There's some coal in that hole," exclaimed Tommy looking back down the hollow that he'd just exited. "I seen a good bit behind those bushes an' I'll bet we could get enough for a few weeks if we wanted."

Their father was one of the many coal miners in the community left unemployed after the last pit closure. Like scores of his fellow workers, Buddy was currently away from home, gone west to Alberta, looking to start a new home for his family. While they waited to join him, living as best they could on what money he was able to send, the whole family sought ways to help out. Blueberries and coal would be welcome.

"Let me have a look," said Karen, appraising the situation. At fifteen, she took her role as the eldest seriously. From the edge of the depression, she peered into the bushes.

"You can't see much from here," offered Tommy. "You gotta go in the hole an' look behind the bushes."

Karen cautiously climbed into the hollow, picking her way through the brambles, carefully parting the leaves with her hands. Sharp branches scratched lightly against her bare legs. It was August, and a warm day, so she and the boys wore cut-off shorts and light t-shirts.

"What do you see?" asked Bobby. "I want to come down, too."

"You stay there, Bobby," replied his sister sternly. "Remember what Ma told us about these holes."

"I know," griped Bobby, rolling his eyes. He mimicked his mother's tone and cadence. "If you gotta look in one 'a them holes, make sure you got someone watching in case there's a cave-in."

About two metres into the cavity, Karen spread the blueberry bushes apart and peered at the ground. Black and shiny, it looked to be a good seam of coal, right at the surface.

"Yer right Tommy," she yelled, "We better tell Ma. This looks like enough for a while." She gave the ground a few stomps with her right foot. "It sounds pretty solid, too. Let's finish with the berries and get home. Maybe we can come back tomorrow with some diggin' tools."

Bobby grasped his sister's extended hand and helped pull her out of the depression, briefly staring at her arm before letting go. "Yer nothin' but skin and bones, Karen," he said shaking his head. "Ma's right, you better start eatin' or you'll get sick."

"You mind yer own business, Bobby," replied Karen. "I'm just fine!" She brushed some leaves out of her hair with her fingers. "I'm not too skinny; I'm slim."

"Karen! Bobby! Over here!" hollered Tommy interrupting. "Look what I found!"

Following Tommy's voice, Karen and Bobby crested a small hill. He was proudly holding up a fifteen centimetre garter snake he'd found under a rock. "Pretty neat, huh?"

"Tommy, you're supposed to be pickin' berries," sighed Karen, noting that the cup by his feet contained only a bottom full. This happened a lot. Tommy loved to play. All the time. His teachers were forever calling home, complaining about his lack of effort. Whenever work was mentioned, Tommy found ways to hide.

"I'll find 'em and you pick 'em," he replied with a grin. "Here, catch," he said, impulsively throwing the little snake in his sister's direction.

Before Karen could scream, Bobby intercepted, catching the wiggling reptile in his left hand. "Come on, be serious, Tommy," he advised. "You gotta learn to help out."

"Like you do?" Tommy retorted sarcastically.

Bobby's face reddened with embarrassment.

"That was a mistake," Karen interjected. "He was trying to help Ma."

A week ago, Bobby had been caught shoplifting; he'd stuffed several candy bars in his pocket and tried to leave the neighborhood store without paying. When caught, he told Mr. Gillis that the treats were for his family, not for himself. The storeowner, who knew of the family's difficulties, didn't press charges, but he did talk to Bobby's mother.

At home, Bobby stuck to his story, even though his mom found evidence of other thefts. Bar and candy wrappers and baseball cards discovered under his bed looked very suspicious, as there was no money to buy those things.

"I sold some berries, Ma," he had pleaded, not convincing anyone.

"If there's any more of this, Bobby, I'll make you tell your father over the phone," she'd warned before confining him to his room for the rest of the day.

Of course, Tommy had overheard the entire exchange.

The siblings filled a second large ice cream container with blueberries before heading home, a fifteen-minute hike. As usual, Tommy ran ahead.

Their house was old and needed paint. It was a company house, a duplex, built for miners' families by the Mining Company during the boom days of the 1920s. There were three bedrooms upstairs and a bathroom with a new shower. The kitchen, with its coal stove, and the family room, containing a coal heater, were on the first floor. Off the hall, leading in from the front porch, was a small washroom. Every room needed paint or new wallpaper but until their father got a full time job, the family lived on whatever he could send home and their mom could raise. There just wasn't extra money for house repairs.

However, it was clean. Their mom insisted on that, stating that soap and water and elbow grease didn't cost much and a clean house demonstrated self-respect and appreciation for what they did have.

"So, Ma," continued Karen, "there's a real good vein of coal visible in that old pit. If we use Tommy's wagon, I think we could stockpile enough for a good part of the winter."

Rose MacDonald was a practical woman; she had to be. In the last ten years, the coal industry had undergone a steady disintegration, leaving many families without any regular income.

The money Buddy sent home wasn't enough to meet all the family expenses, so she had taken a part-time housecleaning position to bring in more cash. This helped with bills and groceries, but she missed her kids and was always tired. If times weren't so tough, she'd have never agreed to such a request.

"Okay, Karen," she sighed, "if you think it's good coal, then bring some home. It'll save us on heating expenses for the winter. But you have to be careful; some of those bootleg mines aren't safe. They go deeper than you think."

"Don't worry, Ma," reassured Karen, "I'll watch close."

Rose nodded reluctantly, then forced her tired, slightly overweight body out of her kitchen chair and patted Karen's shoulder affectionately.

"It is good coal, Ma, I know it is," emphasized Karen, pleased to be contributing.

"Thanks, hon, you're a good help."

"Well, Ma, you can't do it all."

Smiling at her eldest, who now stood eye to eye with her, Rose nodded at the truth of her statement, noting the full sink of dirty dishes. She sighed loudly.

"I know you had a busy day, Karen, but will you bring in the laundry from the line? I didn't get back to it yet and if I'm gonna start those blueberry muffins and pies, like I promised, I'll need some help."

"Sure, Ma," her daughter replied. "I'll fold it and put the basket in the back porch. Then, I'm going over to Brenda's for a bit. Is that okay with you?"

"Sure, dear. That's fine," Rose answered. She turned on the water and squirted some dishwashing liquid into the kitchen sink. "Bobby! Come in here, please. I need you to dry the dishes."

There were a few low murmurs from the living room before her eleven-year-old walked into the kitchen. "Okay,

Ma, I'll help." He was being especially agreeable this week, after the shoplifting episode.

"Tommy, you come help, too," Rose hollered.

The back door slammed as she finished her request. "Figures," she thought, "that boy can smell when someone wants him to work." She turned to the dishes and began her task distractedly, her mind on the laziness of her youngest. Glasses and plates clattered noisily and water splashed. "God knows, Buddy and I are hard workers," she murmured aloud.

"Is everythin' okay, Ma?" asked Bobby, busily drying a plate beside her.

"Just thinkin' out loud," she replied.

After finishing the dishes, she wiped the kitchen table, all the while thinking about Tommy. Fifteen times in detention this past school year! Saucy, won't do his work, refuses to read, class clown … it was very hard to understand where that type of behaviour came from. Tommy was better at home, but he was still very lazy. She shook her head, thinking, "He's only seven; there's still lots of time to grow up."

"All done, Ma," interrupted Bobby, as he put away the last piece of silverware.

"Thank you, Bobby," she smiled, "that was a great help." He beamed at the compliment, and headed toward the back door.

"I'll go find Tommy."

Through the kitchen window, Rose watched Bobby running down the street. He was an average boy who did okay in school, loved sports and, until Buddy went away, never seemed to cause any trouble. A frown creased her brow as she thought of his lying of late—and now this stealing.

"Buddy, I need you," she sighed, turning away to start her promised desserts. "I hope things start turning around soon …."

Rose always found peacefulness in her baking, as she mixed and created delicacies for her family. It helped her relax and kept her mind occupied, although it did create more dirty dishes.

After placing a second tray of blueberry muffins in the oven and moving her unbaked blueberry pie to the fridge, she looked in the family room, hoping to find some help. It was empty, and Karen didn't answer as Rose hollered her name.

"I guess she's already gone to her friend's," murmured Rose, "and the boys are still out." Sighing again, she turned back toward the kitchen. A light shining through the wide-open washroom door caused her to detour. Those kids knew better than to waste electricity. Reaching for the light switch, she saw the toilet seat cover was up and after moving closer, a few food particles floating in the bowl. Rose immediately knew who was responsible — Karen.

Her eldest child was showing definite signs of an eating disorder. A recent television talk show on anorexia nervosa had described her perfectly. Karen was sometimes skipping meals and she'd lost at least eight or nine kilograms in the last three months, but she refused to go to a doctor, denying any problem. "So I had the flu, Ma, that's all. You worry too much."

With tears brimming, Rose flushed away the latest evidence. What else could she do? How could she make Karen stop? If she told Buddy about these problems, he'd want to come home and they just couldn't afford that.

"I hope he gets some steady work soon," she prayed, drying her eyes.

The day dawned bright and windless, showing promise of being another warm one. All three MacDonald children were up and out early to gather the coal they'd discovered. Rose insisted they wear old jeans and sneakers rather than their usual sandals and shorts, knowing how dirty the work would be. She'd also ensured that they ate a good breakfast before leaving — even Karen.

While the two eldest understood and accepted the need for coal, Tommy once again was displaying his usual reluctance to work. "How come I have to pull this thing?" he complained, looking over his shoulder at the battered red wagon trailing behind him.

"Well, it's yer wagon, and it's yer turn to do some helpin'," said Bobby, irritated. "And if I remember correctly, it was you who found the coal!"

Tommy harrumphed loudly, but said nothing further.

"Let's not argue," requested Karen, walking beside the wagon. She checked the tools it contained — work gloves, a pick and two shovels — and did some quick calculations in her head. "Look," she said emphatically, "it will probably take ten or twenty trips to get enough coal to do any good, so we better try and get along." It was only 8 a.m.; they had lots of time to make several trips.

"Here then," shouted Tommy, dropping the wagon handle, "you take a turn."

Bobby looked at him. "Yer so lazy!"

"Well, at least I don't steal," came the over-the-shoulder reply.

Bobby took off after his fast-escaping brother. "When I catch you, yer gonna get it!" he shouted.

"So much for gettin' along," Karen muttered. She picked up the handle and followed the boys into the field. As they got closer to the site, the bushes and brambles got thicker, making it difficult to navigate the wagon. Frustrated, she shouted, "Hey, you two, wait up!"

During the next three hours, despite their differences, the trio managed to deliver four full wagonloads of coal to the bin at the back of their home. Bobby and Tommy did most of the pick and shovel work, while Karen pulled the wagon back and forth. The seam of coal was a good one, with rock that looked clean and pure.

"One more trip before lunch," announced Karen when the wagon was emptied. Their Ma was at work today, so that put her in charge.

"I gotta go to the bathroom," said Bobby, walking toward the back door. "You two go ahead; I'll catch up."

Tommy and Karen started back to Fox Farm, while Bobby went inside. Going to the washroom was just an excuse. He was hungry and had no intention of waiting until lunch. He hurriedly searched through the kitchen cupboards, sampling some of his mother's baking supplies before finding the jackpot — a bag of fresh blueberry muffins. He gobbled two, then gulped a drink of tap water, before hurrying to catch his siblings.

As he jogged up to Karen, she noticed some crumbs on his chin. "What were you into?" she asked suspiciously.

"Nothin'," he lied, "I just used the bathroom."

Karen frowned. Lately, when Bobby looked defiantly at her, as he was doing now, there was no getting the truth out of him. "Well, there's crumbs on yer chin," she stated, hoping for an honest answer. He just ignored her, walking in silence the remaining distance to the field.

Tommy got to the waiting tools first, anxious to finish this last load. He jabbed the spade into the ground a few times to soften the coal. "Hey — there's a hole here," he hollered excitedly, "... a tunnel!"

Karen and Bobby rushed to join their brother in the depression. They had removed most of the bushes overlying the seam of coal earlier that morning, making it easy to see what was attracting Tommy's attention. The hole was at the back of the cleared section, about the width of the shovel.

Blueberries and Coal & Inside the Triangle   13

"Be careful, Tommy," warned Karen, but Tommy wasn't listening. He was rattling the spade in and out of the opening excitedly, trying to make it wider. Both older children moved to stop him, recognizing the risk he was taking, yet forgetting to leave a lookout.

"Stop, Tommy!" shouted Bobby.

As they reached him, the ground began to shudder and shake. Instinctively, Karen grabbed Tommy, turning him around, while Bobby seized his other hand.

They were too late.

The earth around them fell inward, swallowing the trio in a haze of dust and a rumble of noise. Frantically, they clawed at the earth to gain a hold, trying to stop their descent, but to no avail. In seconds, surrounded by falling rock and dirt, they were sliding and rolling down a steep incline into the depths of the mine.

Their shrieks were masked by the deep rumbling of the slide. Thick dust filled their eyes, noses, and mouths, and rocks battered their bodies. To the frightened siblings, the fifteen-second tumble seemed like forever.

Three

Heavy silence filled the deep cavern, broken intermittently by soft sobbing and faint moans. Dim light suffused the thick, dust-filled air, tentative rays filtering down from a small opening high above.

"Bobby, Tommy," called Karen in a carefully controlled voice, "Are you guys okay?" She hurt everywhere from the long tumble and falling rocks, but could move all her limbs.

"I'm okay," sputtered Bobby, coughing from the darkness to her left. "Just banged up a bit."

"Me, too," piped Tommy from behind Karen, his voice quivering. "I didn't mean to — I didn't think … I'm sorry," he sobbed.

"That's no never mind now, Tommy," said Karen softly, as she crawled carefully toward his voice. "Wave your arms and I'll find you. Bobby, you stay put," she added. "We gotta stay close."

"Yer almost here, Karen," said Tommy, relief evident in his voice. "I can hear you real good."

Karen reached out to the sound of her brother's voice, grasped his waving arm and pulled him close in a comforting hug. "I was so scared," he whispered tearfully.

"We're gonna be okay," Karen reassured. "Let's go find Bobby."

"You stay where yer at," his voice directed. "It's easier for me to come to you two. Just keep talkin'."

In less than a minute, his hand found Tommy's back. "Just like Ma warned us," he said, embracing his siblings. "These old pits can be a lot deeper than you think."

As the dust settled and their eyes adapted to the surrounding darkness, they could make out each other's silhouette.

"What are we gonna do, Karen?" asked Bobby. "We can't climb back up there." The faint light in their darkened sky looked to be thirty metres or more above them.

"We have to wait here," she replied practically. "Ma knows where we went today. When she gets home from work, she'll start lookin'. She'll get neighbors to help find us, and they'll see our tools and wagon …."

"Yeah," interjected Bobby, "they'll be here later today or at the latest in the morning."

"You mean we have to stay here in the dark until tomorrow?" asked Tommy, pushing closer to his big sister. "I don't like it here."

"We're gonna be okay, Tommy," repeated Karen reassuringly. "We're together and nobody's hurt, so don't worry."

Listening, Bobby stared at his sister's outline, surprised that her movements were so visible. "Hey, there's some kind of light behind you, Karen," he whispered. "Like a faint glowin' …."

Sure enough, a dull shimmering of green radiated softly from the direction Bobby indicated.

"The walls of the cave must be fluorescent," said Karen. She had learned of such things in her Grade 9 science class. "You know, like Ma's alarm clock."

Quickly forgetting his nervousness, Tommy struggled to his feet. "Hey, let's go see," he exclaimed, tugging on his sister's hand.

"Hold it, mister," Karen retorted, tightening her grip. "We stay together."

"Do you think it's safe?" asked Bobby. "Maybe it's radioactive," he added, recalling a story from his science fiction collection.

"Maybe somebody *lives* down here," added Tommy. "Maybe a mutant monster ...."

"Stop it, you two," ordered Karen, "It's just fluorescence."

A long silence followed her words.

"All right," she sighed to the unspoken question, "Let's go look."

Slowly they made their way toward the luminescence, avoiding, as best they could, the rocks strewn over the cave floor. Karen stayed in the middle, holding her brothers' hands, at times having to pull Tommy back. The greenish glow took on an oval shape as they neared, illuminating a cavern extending beyond.

"That's so cool," whispered Bobby.

"Let's put some rocks here in the shape of an arrow," suggested Karen as they reached the cavern entrance. "It'll show us the way back, and let any searchers know where we've gone."

The boys quickly set about gathering rocks, making thunderous echoes as they dropped them in place.

"Wow," admired Karen, standing at the entrance. "This is beautiful!"

"It's creepy, if you ask me," replied Tommy, still half expecting the alien monster to appear.

Bobby walked slowly into the shadowy cavern, scanning the walls for openings or tunnels. His feet scuffed the ground, sending pebbles scooting forward. A metallic twang caught

Blueberries and Coal & Inside the Triangle   **17**

his attention, diverting his gaze from the walls to the rough, uneven floor. Karen and Tommy watched curiously as Bobby bent to retrieve an object.

"It looks like a compass," he exclaimed, squinting in the faint light. Twisting the round disc from side to side and rotating it in his palm, he noted the face had the same green glow as the cavern walls. "There's funny markings, though," he added as his siblings gathered near. "Look, there's an H at the top, at the 12 o'clock spot, and an L at 6 o'clock." He twisted it to get a better view. "An' there's an arrow pointing left of the H near 10 o'clock." He twisted it back and forth but the arrow stayed steady. "Weird."

"Now, what could that be about?" Karen queried, turning the little disc over.

"Useless, if you ask me," Tommy uttered, quickly losing interest.

"Maybe you should keep it, Bobby," Karen offered thoughtfully, passing it back.

"Yeah, you can prob'ly sell it when we get home," Tommy suggested, moving forward into the illuminated chamber.

Bobby slipped the compass into his back pocket and started after his younger brother. Curving jaggedly toward their left, the shadowy walls invited exploration, with several large boulders just asking to be climbed.

"Stay in sight, Tommy," shouted Karen, feeling awed by this underground beauty. She walked slowly in the direction the boys now moved. Beneath her foot, a crunching noise caused her to pause. Bending, she noticed sparkles of flashing light reflected from a small rectangle. "It's a mirror," she exclaimed, grasping it by a thin handle.

"It's probably a signal mirror," suggested Bobby, turning back to look.

"Maybe," Karen answered, twirling its handle. "But it looks kind'a delicate for mining work."

"An' it's just what you need, Karen," Bobby joked, laughing a little. "Yer hair's a mess."

"Come on, you guys," called Tommy impatiently, looking over his shoulder from atop a large boulder. "We'll never get anywhere if you don't hurry up."

"Tommy, get down from there," hollered Karen looking up from the mirror. Predictably, the warning was too late. As he stepped forward, Tommy slipped, sliding off the smooth surface of the boulder to the rough ground below.

"Oooowww! I'm bleedin'," he howled, holding up his hand.

As his siblings rushed toward him, Tommy's cries abruptly stopped. Sitting up, he triumphantly held something above his head. "What d'ya know?" he exclaimed, grinning widely, "I found something, too." He examined it closely. "It's a chisel … I cut my hand on a chisel. Who'd throw away such a neat tool?"

His injuries forgotten, he offered Bobby his new tool. "It's probably diamond tipped," he enthused, his imagination soaring. "See how it glitters?"

"You better be careful with this," cautioned his brother.

"I bet I can use it to help dig us out of here," Tommy replied, taking the chisel back from his brother. "An' fight off any green eyed goblins!" He made a few sword-like swipes with it before stuffing it into his rear pants pocket.

"Let me see your hand," Karen instructed, ignoring her brother's over active imagination. She grasped his arm and carefully surveyed the damage, finding a very minor puncture on his left thumb. "You sure made a lot of noise for such a tiny hole," she muttered.

Tommy glared at her.

"This place is pretty big," said Bobby, a few meters ahead of his sibling. He was slowly turning in a circle taking in the cracks and crevices of the walls and ceiling.

Blueberries and Coal & Inside the Triangle

"Yeah, we better not go too far in," cautioned Karen, "or we won't be able to hear the rescuers when they come."

"Well, why don't we ...?" started Bobby.

"Look over there," interrupted Tommy, once again bouncing out in front. He was pointing to their left. "I think I see train tracks."

Sure enough, as they rounded an outcropping of rock, a set of tracks crossed their path, reaching into deep tunnels on either side. "This must have been a pretty big operation in its day if they needed train cars for the coal and miners," stated Tommy, wonder in his tone.

"And — the tracks have to lead out," Bobby added excitedly.

To the right, the tracks descended deeper into the earth, while the left route stretched flat and fairly straight into the distance. The eerie green light seemed to extend endlessly in both directions. Naturally, they chose the tracks leading left, with Tommy, as usual, running ahead.

"Look, you guys," he called, "a sign."

"What does it say?" asked Karen, stooping to make a second arrow marking their trail.

"I dunno," answered Tommy.

"It says *The Help Yourself Rail*," read Bobby, leaning over Tommy's shoulder.

"Hah! That's a neat name for a bootleg coal business," laughed Tommy.

"Tommy, why couldn't you read that?" asked Bobby.

"The light's too dim; I can't make out all the letters."

"Maybe if you'd practice readin' at home, you'd have been able to read it," Karen scolded, rejoining her brothers. "Every time Ma gets out a book, you take off."

"Practice makes perfect," added Bobby.

"Well, you two ain't so perfect, either," retorted Tommy defensively. "Miss Skinny's always lookin' at herself in the mirror, while you," he pointed at Bobby, "been stealin' things." With that, he broke into a run, knowing he was in for trouble.

"You little brat, get back here," shouted Karen, just missing his arm.

Bobby angrily chased after his younger brother, quickly gaining ground. Seeing his pursuer, Tommy hollered, "I didn't mean it ... I didn't mean it!"

The boys sped along the tracks and around a small curve, stopping in mid-stride, both their mouths gaping in surprise. In front of them was a small miners' transport train, glowing with the same strange colour as the walls of the cave. It looked more like a roller coaster than a real train, with three passenger seats linked together but no engine. An upright lever, probably a brake, was attached on the left of the lead car.

"Wow," gasped Tommy and Bobby together, both more interested in the train than their recent disagreement. Karen joined them, her breathing heavy from running. "Don't you two ever take off like that again," she scolded. Then she, too, saw the little train. "Oh my gosh ...."

Emblazoned on the side of each car, in fancy gold lettering, was the train's name. *"The Help Yourself Train,"* said Tommy.

"That's *Rail,* not *Train,"* corrected Karen. "You *do* need to practice reading," she muttered, more to herself than Bobby. She didn't want another argument.

"Why don't we stay here for the night?" suggested Bobby. "Those cars are just wide enough to lie down in, and we can each have our own."

Tommy jumped into the lead car. "This one's mine," he laughed. "I'm the engineer."

"Figures," sighed Karen, rolling her eyes skyward. "Okay," she said aloud. "Bobby, you take the middle one and I'll go in back."

"Ha, Karen, you got the caboose," shouted Tommy gleefully.

Blueberries and Coal & Inside the Triangle   21

Bobby stretched out in the middle car, grateful for the rest.

None of the MacDonald children owned a watch, but Karen figured it must be nearing 4:00 or 5:00 p.m. "Ma should be getting home soon," she said. "People'll be out lookin' for us first thing."

"I hope so," Bobby said gloomily. "I'm hungry."

"Well, at least you had some muffins," Karen replied pointedly.

He glared at her. "Leave me alone."

There was no further conversation. The three children were all tired, hungry, and irritable. Understandable given the circumstances but lately, it seemed, any conversation resulted in a disagreement or hurt feelings.

Before lying down, Karen surveyed her car. The cushions were soft and comfortable, surprisingly free of dust or grime. Even underneath her seat was clean—and without bugs! Despite her anxieties, she *was* tired. She curled up on her side, with her knees tucked into her chest.

Bobby stretched his arms and legs, working out the kinks and aches. It had been a long day. He snuggled into his cushioned seat, yawning widely.

Tommy, a bit sleepy, was still too curious about the train to rest. He searched every centimetre of his car, inside and out, for any secret compartments or dropped tools, but didn't find anything. "Where's the engine?" he wondered. "It's no good havin' a train that can't go nowhere."

He noted a squeeze handle at the top of the brake. "Useless thing," he thought, reaching for it. "What's the use of a brake, when the train can't move?" Impulsively, he squeezed the handle and pushed it forward. With loud squealing and screeching, the train jerked forward. "We're on a level," he shouted, shocked at what he'd caused. "We can't go nowhere!"

"Karen, Bobby, wake up!" he screamed, squirming around in his seat. "We're movin'!" Neither of his siblings stirred.

His heart pounding, Tommy briefly considered jumping off, but what would happen to Karen and Bobby? Frantically, he grabbed the lever and pulled it back, hoping to undo his error. The train jerked and shuddered, sending high-pitched, shrieking noises into the tunnel, but didn't slow. Crying, Tommy slumped down in his seat, alone with his guilt and worry. The rhythmic clickety clack of the train drained his energy and despite his upset, Tommy was soon fast asleep.

The Help Yourself Rail accelerated, navigating many curves and several hills, the sleeping passengers oblivious to their progress.

CLANG! Karen's car was released at its destination.

CLANK! Bobby's car was delivered.

CLUNK! Tommy came to a sudden stop.

They had all arrived ... But where?

Four

Loud squealing startled Tommy awake as his rail car jerked to a stop. Sitting up, he shook his head and looked out at totally unfamiliar surroundings — and bright sunlight. "What's goin' on?" he sputtered.

Cobwebs clouded his thoughts but he knew he should still be in the mine. His heart pounded and panic welled, bringing tears to his eyes. Karen and Bobby were nowhere in sight — and neither were their railcars!

He sniffled, drying his eyes on his sleeve. Why was he always getting himself in trouble? If only he had been more cautious before pushing that lever. He glared angrily at the brake.

Music was playing and, surprisingly, Tommy recognized the melody. It reminded him of the circus … of … merry–go–round music. Curious, he gazed in the direction of the sound, beyond a small grassy hill to his right. Maybe there were people there, he hoped; maybe even his brother and sister.

Twisting in his seat, he scouted every direction. Tracks that exited the cave opening behind him stretched up a steep hill into towering mountains. A solid rock wall, carved from the mountainside itself, blocked the left, leaving only one way to explore.

Jumping from his perch, Tommy spied a rectangular road sign at the base of the hill. Scurrying over, he studied the printed black letters, but couldn't decipher the words:

> REMAIN IN THE CAR
> IF YOU DON'T WANT TO STAY
> BUT GET OUT
> AND THE CAR GOES AWAY

Screeching wheels interrupted his deliberation. *The Help Yourself Rail* car was moving, accelerating forward.

"Get back here!" Tommy hollered, running toward the car. As it sped up the hill, shrinking into the distance, he howled loudly in disappointment, his hands tightly fisted. Frustrated, and not knowing what else to do or where else to go, he turned back toward the music. As he passed the road sign, he gave it an angry kick, knocking it to the ground.

"Stupid sign," he muttered, "it's because of you I got out of the car." His aggression didn't help; he was still lost, and alone, and now his big toe was throbbing. Nothing was going right.

The lively music continued, undisturbed by his outburst, enticing and promising. He kept walking. As he crested a small grassy hill, the largest circus he could ever have imagined stretched out in all directions. Eyes wide, he laughed aloud with glee. There were sparkling rides of every kind, shape, and size almost as far as he could see. Delicious smells of cotton candy and popcorn wafted upward from a high stone wall surrounding the park.

"How do you get in?" Tommy wondered aloud, his stomach rumbling. From his vantage atop the crest, he searched for an entrance. The granite barrier, several times Tommy's height, showed no visible break or opening. He drifted closer, moving down the slight hill toward his left.

The fields surrounding the circus were spotted with brightly coloured wild flowers. Long, gently swaying grass extended all the way down to the wall, abruptly turning to dirt. Further off to the left, impossible to miss, Tommy spied a lone redwood marking a corner of the wall. The massive tree dwarfed the barricade with its six metre girth and seventy metre height.

Looking skyward at the giant tree, Tommy whistled in awe.

Up close, it was even more impressive, overpowering everything in its immediate area. Passing beyond the massive trunk, Tommy squealed excitedly. Previously hidden behind the big tree, a huge red slide filled his view, stretching from the crest of another hill over the wall into the circus below.

"Aha," he laughed, "a way in."

Impatiently, he scrambled up the grassy incline to the slide. A small sign with bright red lettering was posted beside the entrance steps. Tommy, unable to make out any of the words, passed it with disdain.

> NOTICE: THIS PARK HAS NO EXIT.
> ONLY ENTER IF YOU PLAN ON STAYING!

He eagerly climbed the ladder, counting thirty steps to the top of the slide. Brightly coloured tents and rides were everywhere. Even from a distance, Tommy recognized the Ferris wheel, scrambler, a merry–go–round, and several roller coasters.

"This is gonna be awesome," he thought, pushing forward onto the slide. "But where are all the people?"

FIVE

Bobby stretched his arms upward and slowly opened his eyes, expecting darkness. "Wh ... what the heck happened?" he stammered, jerking to a sitting position. Squinting from the bright sunlight, he noted people walking back and forth beside his rail car. Aside from an occasional brief glance, most seemed to avoid his gaze, and no one spoke. Beyond the passersby stood a long, low building, sporting a bright sign that read *'Rail Station.'*

He swiveled about, looking for his siblings. An old locomotive and a few coal cars were off to his left, but no small cars like his were anywhere along the tracks in either direction.

Panicked, he waved and tried to make eye contact with people that passed. "Hey, mister, did you see ...? Ma'am, where ...?"

They looked away, pointedly ignoring him. "What's wrong with you?" he shouted, angry at their rudeness. "I need help!" His voice trailed to a whisper and his head slumped forward. Through tear-filled eyes, he noticed how filthy he was; coal dust stained his hands, arms, and clothing. His t–shirt was torn on the right shoulder, his jeans thread-worn and frayed.

"I look a mess," he thought, acutely self-conscious. "Maybe that's why nobody's helpin' me."

People gave him wide berth as he climbed onto the receiving platform and headed toward the station to find a washroom. Halfway to the entrance, sharp squealing filled the air as his rail car lurched forward.

"Noooo!" he shouted, scrambling back in a futile chase.

Standing still, fists clenched in frustration, Bobby watched the car disappear in the distance. "Great," he thought sarcastically, "now I'm stuck here."

Dejected, his gaze leveled downward, he slowly shuffled to the station building. A woman hurrying by almost collided with him, veering away at the last moment. "Watch where you're going, young man," she reprimanded.

Bobby sneered at her retreating figure. "Friendly place," he muttered. An older woman at the station entrance watched him approach.

"Excuse me, ma'am, could you tell me the name of this place?"

The woman looked at him disapprovingly, making a show of noting the coal stains in his hair, on his face, and on his clothes. Her expression irritated Bobby, reminding him of the kids at school. They looked at him like that sometimes, like they were better than him because they had nicer clothes and more money. Being poor, he got used to such treatment, but it never felt good.

"Do you live around here?" the woman asked in a haughty voice. "We don't allow vagrants into Rail Town, you know."

Bobby stared at her. "I'm no vagrant," he replied. "I fell asleep on the train and missed my stop," he fibbed. "I work in the pit with my father and we live in Coal Town," he added. "I just want to get cleaned up, get some food, and go home."

"Well, there's a washroom in there," the woman said, waving her hand in the general direction of the entrance. "And I do hope you have some other clothes because, if the mayor sees you walking around looking like *that*," she made a disgusted face, "he'll have you put in poorman's jail for sure."

Bobby's temper flared. "If everybody is like you here, it must be a real miserable place to live," he retorted icily. The woman gasped, shocked by his words.

He didn't care. She deserved it; they all did. Neither that woman, nor anyone else, had any right judging him on his appearance. Seething with anger, he entered the train station and the bathroom. "I hate being poor!" he thought, slamming his fist down on the sink counter. Tears tracked clean streaks down his blackened face.

He abruptly turned on the taps, water splashing from the sink over his shirt and pants. Cupping his hands, he doused his face, the sudden coldness soothing his anger.

"I do look pretty bad," he admitted, studying his reflection in the mirror above the sink. His light brown hair was totally blackened with coal dust, and his clothes ... well, his mom wouldn't have been happy. Using the liquid soap dispenser beside the taps, Bobby washed his hair and exposed skin, his mood improving as the dirt disappeared. Twisting to see if his ears were clean, he glimpsed a garment bag hanging from a hook on the washroom door.

"Wonder what that is?" he murmured, curious. He dried his hands and glanced in all directions. After ensuring that no one else was in the washroom, he grabbed the bag and unzipped it, discovering a colourful Hawaiian shirt, a cool pair of Levi black denims, and some Nike sneakers with new gym socks stuffed into the toes.

Reflexively, he checked the sizes, delighted that everything would fit him. "Maybe my luck is changing," he muttered, removing the garment bag from its hook. "That woman was right — I'm gonna get thrown in that poorman's jail if I go out like this," he reasoned to his reflection. "Why, I bet this stuff has been here a long time and someone's prob'ly gonna throw it out soon. So if I take it, it won't hurt nobody … and I really do need it."

He opened the washroom door slightly, checking for traffic. Nobody was coming, so he hustled the garment bag into the washroom stall and hung it on the door. His heart was pounding; he'd never taken anything so big or expensive before. Sure, he'd pocketed some candy and small toys, and even some loose change, but never anything like this.

As he removed his dirty clothing, the forgotten "compass" fell to the floor with a clatter. He quickly picked it up to stifle the noise and re-examined the tin casing. It was shiny and smooth, with very little sign of previous use. When he turned it face up, the arrow still pointed to the left of the H, a little further than before, now between nine and ten o'clock.

"Weird," he thought, placing the compass on the back of the toilet while he finished dressing.

Everything fit perfectly. Bobby gazed with satisfaction at his transformation in the mirror. "The kids at home wouldn't laugh now," he thought vainly, putting the garment bag filled with his old clothes back on the hook.

Before leaving the washroom, he retrieved his compass. The arrow had moved again, now pointing midway between the H and L. "That's funny," he muttered. "Nothin' happened to make it move." He carefully put it in his back pocket, then headed to the door, very pleased with his cool clothes.

He wasn't going to any poorman's jail.

SIX

Karen usually took a few minutes to fully awaken, but not today. Memories of the cave-in flooded her thoughts, quickly clearing her mind as she opened her eyes. The surroundings were changed; there were lights and it was noisy. "What happened?" she wondered with confusion and a twinge of fear, swiveling about to find her brothers. Her rail car was in some type of underground station with a large commuter train in front of it. "This must be a subway!" she realized anxiously. "I'm in a city."

"Hey, you! You down there!" A short, thin, elderly man on the exit platform above waved his arms, trying to get her attention.

Karen met his gaze. "The next train is due any minute, Miss," he hollered. "You'd better get out of there unless you want to get run over!"

The train in front *was* pulling away, and a quick glance over her shoulder confirmed that, indeed, another was approaching. The little man gestured toward an iron ladder attached to the side of the subway platform beside Karen's little car. Nodding her understanding, she fluidly climbed from her rail car to the cast iron steps. As she reached the top rung, the rail car sped off into the subway tunnel.

"Oh, no!" she gasped, realizing she was stranded.

A hand grasped her forearm and helped her up the last step, steadying her until she gained her bearings. The white-haired gentleman, no taller than Karen, smiled welcomingly with straight white teeth.

"Where did you come from, Miss? You look like you were in a dust storm or something."

Self-consciously, Karen noted her disheveled appearance. Head to toe, she was caked with black grime. "We had an accident. M ... my brothers and I were ... ." Tears welled up and her voice quivered to a stop.

The old man wordlessly took her hand and led her to a nearby bench. Simultaneously, passengers from the next train filled the platform, giving Karen a few moments to compose herself.

By the time the crowd thinned, she had better control of her emotions. Clearing her throat, she turned to her new acquaintance. "I ... I don't really know how I got here," she began truthfully. "My two brothers were with me, and we got trapped in an old coal mine. There were some cars in a clearing — *The Help Yourself Rail* — and we each got into one. I fell asleep and just woke up here when you were calling me."

The man's expression didn't change during Karen's brief explanation. His eyes, an intense blue, showed concern without any sign of surprise or doubt. "This must be quite a shock, then," he soothed, passing her a handkerchief. "Why don't you come home with me to get cleaned up?"

Karen stiffened and moved to get up. While the old gentleman seemed nice enough, he was a stranger. "I don't think ...."

Her elderly companion immediately understood her concern. "My wife would probably love a little company," he interjected, "and I bet she has some clean clothes, as well."

Karen relaxed a bit, but remained standing.

"And perhaps a little food?" he added. "Mabel, my wife, is such a good cook."

His smile looked genuine and his manner exuded calm. Karen realized she needed help, but should she trust this man? For some reason, she felt safe with him, almost like she'd met him before.

She nodded, accepting his offer.

Her guide stood and offered Karen his arm. "Shall we?" he smiled, leading her to the subway exit. "It's just a short walk."

They made a strange pair: an old man dressed in clean slacks and a white, short-sleeved shirt, and a coal-coated young lady.

"I'm Karen," she offered as they climbed a set of winding stairs.

"Hi, Karen," the old man smiled. "You can call me Gus."

The two emerged from the stairway onto a busy downtown street. Karen had never seen such tall buildings or so much traffic, and people were everywhere. A few passing faces registered Karen's filthy appearance, causing Gus to laugh aloud. "People are so rude," he observed.

Reveling in the busy scene, Karen barely noticed the impolite glances. Pivoting, she drank in the cosmopolitan air, noting people of all heights and races, wearing varying fashion and hairstyles. But there was something odd ....

"Gus, am I imaginin' things, or are all these people really thin?" she asked.

"Thin?" he paused and thought for a moment. "No, these are all pretty normal people. Hardly anyone in the city gains weight like you," he said innocently.

Karen stopped walking. "What?" she asked incredulously. His answer described her own view of her body size, but she didn't like hearing it. Nobody had ever agreed with her that she was fat; they all said she was too thin!

Blueberries and Coal & Inside the Triangle   **33**

"Oh," replied Gus, "did I say something wrong?"

"No, — not really," Karen answered haltingly. "It's just … well … where I come from, people think I'm skinny."

Gus chuckled. "Let's ask the missus when we get home."

Seven

Whizzing down the slide, twisting and weaving through banks and turns, Tommy squealed with delight. After a breathless turn above the enclosing wall, the far end of the slide came into view. Finishing high above a circular pool, the final drop provided a refreshing entrance to the park.

Whooping and hollering, Tommy soared into the air before crashing, with a loud splash, into the warm water. Mechanical laughter issued from a nearby speaker: "Welcome to the circus. Fun all the time. Fun, fun, fun! Hahahahahahahah."

The water wasn't deep, just reaching Tommy's chest, so he waded easily toward the exit stairs, splashing playfully en route. "What a great entrance," he laughed, still thrilled from the ride and the dunk. "I gotta do that again!"

Behind him, coal dust streamed from his clothes, making black stains in the swirling water. Tommy impulsively ducked his head, vigorously rubbing his hair and face, adding to the spreading cloud.

"Towels and blow dryers in the tent to your left," the mechanical voice directed as Tommy climbed the stairs. "Dry off before proceeding."

"Where's that comin' from?" thought Tommy, searching around. To his left stood a large purple and yellow tent with a canopied entrance; in front, a merry-go round, empty and quiet and, to his right that huge tree … but no speakers anywhere.

He scampered about, exploring his new surroundings, hoping to find some people. Rides were everywhere—but they were all empty!

"Hello!" he shouted, cupping his hands to his mouth. "Anybody here?"

Only the mechanical voice answered, telling him again to go to the purple tent and dry off. Tommy walked around the big tent once before peering through its entrance. Since the cave-in, he was determined to be more careful.

"Maybe everyone's in here," he muttered aloud. Cautiously he stepped inside, listening and watching for any signs of people. After finding a washroom and a locker room, Tommy finally found the 'drying room'. It was filled with fluffy bath towels of every colour, but no people. Disappointed, he grabbed a dark, blue towel and sat dejectedly on a wooden bench.

"Dry off before proceeding."

"Oh, shut up," he grumbled, stripping away his soggy clothes. "Yer startin' to bug me."

Throwing the wet towel aside, he grabbed another, wrapping it around his waist, the edge almost hitting the floor. Using hot air blowers mounted beside the towel racks, he dried his clothes, including his sneakers, muttering and complaining nonstop. After dressing, he threw the second towel to the ground under the blower.

Beside it, glinting in the light was his chisel. "Jeez," Tommy exclaimed, stooping, "I don't wanna lose this!" He waved it around, jabbing in and out, up and down, liking the light that glittered off its tip. Curiously, Tommy noted some letters on the blade that he hadn't seen in the dark coal mine. Rubbing his fingers over the engraving, he thought of his siblings. Oh, how he wished that Karen or Bobby was with him; they'd tell him what the words were and they'd help him get back home. He moodily shoved the chisel back into his pocket and headed outside.

On his own, the merry-go-round didn't interest him, so he bypassed it, wandering deeper into the circus grounds. The rides were operating but there weren't any passengers or workers; everything was mechanized. "Lifeless," thought Tommy, grimacing. Even the jaunty music seemed empty without chatter and laughter.

At the entrance to each ride was a sign:

> FREE RIDE
> FIVE-MINUTE THRILL
> DO IT AGAIN
> HAVE FUN!

Tommy sighed aloud, once again wishing he could read. In grade primary, he'd really tried to learn all his letters, but the different shapes were confusing, and he had a hard time remembering which way they went. The letters *b, p, q* and *d* were the toughest to distinguish, but *w* and *m*, and *u* and *n*, were hard, too. By the middle of first grade, he was very frustrated; Bobby and Karen were good readers and so were his friends, Billy and Allan. Why couldn't he be like them?

He had a good memory, though. When his mom read his homework stories to him, he'd listen, and quickly memorize passages, asking her to repeat the longer sections. He was so good at memorizing that his teacher believed he was actually reading! When she'd ask for a volunteer to read an assigned story aloud, he'd frequently raise his hand … and he always did great. Until that day the teacher and everybody laughed at him. His cheeks burned with shame at the memory.

She'd made him read a story he hadn't practiced, so he made something up from the pictures on the page. Unfortunately, it wasn't even close. Embarrassed, he'd thrown his book and stormed out of the classroom. That resulted in the first of many trips to the principal's office.

From that day on, he simply refused to read aloud. If the teacher insisted, he'd politely decline, then sit quietly at his desk, ignoring her. When she continued to push, he'd make saucy, smart-ass remarks that got everyone laughing. It was different when people laughed *with* him.

Still, he did wish he could read that sign. Maybe it said something important. He knew some of the letters, but that was it. No words. No meaning.

A light breeze tousled his hair, bringing a smell that shattered his melancholy mood. "Popcorn!" he shouted happily, his stomach rumbling.

Following his nose, Tommy entered a green and pink canopied tent, with a giant picture of popcorn above its entrance. A large glass container on a long table was filled with mounds of mouth-watering, golden popcorn. Juice. Pop. Plastic cups and cardboard containers.

Tommy hollered, "Is anybody here? I'd like some service, please."

No answer.

"Hellooo!" he shouted, looking around.

A sign was tacked to the front of the table:

> EAT AND DRINK YOUR FILL
> IT'S ALL FREE
> AT THE CIRCUS

"Not again," he whined. Then, hoping someone might hear, in a loud voice: "Well, I guess I'll just help myself."

But no one came, so Tommy did help himself, eating two full boxes of popcorn and drinking three glasses of orange juice. With a full stomach he felt better, but he was lonely and worried about his siblings. He went back outside to explore and hopefully find some people!

Deeper inside the circus, the rides got more interesting. "Since I'm here," Tommy reasoned, "I might as well try some of these." Hours passed, as he went from ride to ride. His favourite, the Zipper, reminded him of the circuses he'd attended with Bobby in his hometown. This circus was fun, he admitted, but it would be *more* fun with company. He missed his mom, Bobby, even Karen and he wanted to go home.

Wandering erratically through the maze of tents and rides, Tommy found himself in the centre of a food court. Booths offered a variety of choices, judging from the pictures hanging above each counter. Under the pictures were signs containing both letters and numbers. Tommy knew numbers — those must be prices.

"Wow, it looks like I need to pay to get real food," he thought, looking around. He chose a table in front of the pizza booth, wondering how to get service. On one of the three other tables in the food court, he spied an old-fashioned hand bell. Grabbing it, he enthusiastically swung it above his head, liking the clanging noise it made. Unexpectedly, shuffling footsteps resulted. A small, thin man, with a kindly face, bright blue eyes, and a friendly smile entered.

Tommy's eyes widened.

"Hello, young man, can I be of service?"

"Hi ... yes, sir, you can," replied Tommy, fumbling for words. "I'm lost, an' I'm hungry, an' ...." Tears choked off his words.

The old man took Tommy's hand in both of his, led him to a chair and sat beside him. "It's okay to cry when you have such a good reason," he comforted.

Blueberries and Coal & Inside the Triangle   **39**

Still sniffling, Tommy avoided the man's gaze, embarrassed at his outburst.

His companion understood his discomfort. "It's not what I think that matters; right now, it's how *you* feel that's important." He passed Tommy a handkerchief, "We all feel and we all hurt, son."

Tommy lifted his eyes, comforted by the kind words. The old guy's white hair, eyebrows and clean-shaven face reminded him of Grandpa, someone he could trust.

"My name's Tommy," he said, wiping his eyes. "What's yers?"

"Gus."

"I got lost in a coal mine with my brother an' sister, an' we found a train car, an' I released the brake, an' ... I ended up here." His words were running into each other. "I don't know where my brother and sister are."

"Was it *The Help Yourself Rail?*" Gus asked, surprising Tommy.

"Yeah, it was!" he replied excitedly. "You know about it?"

"A little," answered the old man. "Enough to know that your brother and sister are safe." He released Tommy's hand and smiled reassuringly at the boy. "Now," he continued, "are you enjoying the park? I'm the groundskeeper here."

"It's a pretty neat place, but there's nobody else here," Tommy complained. "It'd be more fun if there were people to share it with ... an' I can't see no way out, either."

"Did you notice the sign before you climbed up the entrance slide?"

"Yeah," replied the little boy suspiciously. "Why?"

"Didn't you read it?"

Tommy sensed he should be truthful with Gus, even if it was embarrassing. "No, I didn't," he whispered, blushing. "I can't read."

Gus was silent for a moment. "There's no way out," he finally said. "The exit is blocked by that large tree near the slide. The sign warned you not to come if you didn't want to stay."

"But I didn't know!" shouted Tommy, losing his temper. He anger was directed more toward his inability to read than at Gus, but he wanted to go home. "You better let me out of here!" He was on his feet, both fists clenched.

"I don't make the rules," replied Gus, calmly ignoring Tommy's aggression. "If there are any other questions, you can ask me now — or later."

Tommy wanted to run from the situation, but resisted, this wasn't school. If he didn't listen, he might never get out. He grudgingly sat down again, relaxing his hands, uncertain what to do. Maybe if he had a good meal and some rest, he could figure out a plan.

"Gus, I'm really hungry," he started, gesturing toward the pizza booth. "Can I get some food over there?"

"If you have money, you can," Gus replied.

"Errrr!" Tommy growled.

"Pizza costs money, Tommy, but you can have all the popcorn, cotton candy, and sodas that you want for free. Like the signs say."

Tommy was frustrated. "I don't got no money," he complained, trying to control his voice. "Can I trade this?" he asked, fishing the chisel from his pocket.

"Sorry, no trades."

"Gus, I'm starvin'," Tommy pleaded.

"Hmm," said Gus, rubbing his chin thoughtfully. "Well, I guess you'll have to find a job."

"What?" gaped Tommy in surprise.

"Why, yes," continued Gus. "If you want to eat this food," he pointed to the restaurants, "then you need money — and, to get money, you must earn it."

"But, I'm just a kid. You can't make me work!"

Blueberries and Coal & Inside the Triangle 41

"You're quite right, Tommy, it's entirely up to you. Just like reading, it's your choice."

"Stop talkin' to me like that! You don't know how hard I tried to learn to read," Tommy griped defensively. "It's the teacher's fault; she never taught me the right way."

"No, Tommy, I suspect you gave up when it required some effort," Gus replied, locking eyes with the squirming boy.

"Yer just like everybody else," retorted Tommy, jumping up, tears in his eyes. "You don't understand."

"Yes, I do, Tommy," smiled Gus sadly. "I do understand."

But Tommy wasn't listening; he was too angry.

"An' I don't want no job," he shouted, heading to the exit. "I'm a kid, an' I don't have to do work."

Gus serenely watched Tommy's retreat. "If you change your mind, or there's anything else I can help you with, you know where to find me."

EIGHT

Exiting the washroom, Bobby guiltily surveyed his surroundings, half expecting someone to stop him. Surprisingly, glances from passersby actually seemed friendly, some nodding, and others even smiling. No one recognized his stolen outfit, or his anxiety.

"Ha," he thought with satisfaction, "No poorman's jail for me!"

Still, he'd better avoid that woman.

Impulsively, he sauntered over to the ticket counter. "Excuse me, mister," he said to the man behind the little window, "if I wanted to go someplace, how much would it cost?"

The ticket agent barely even looked up, answering in a monotone, disinterested voice: "It's always the same, no matter where you want to go. Ten dollars."

"Thanks, I'll be back later," Bobby muttered, distractedly moving toward the front entrance. How was he going to find ten dollars to get back home? For that matter, where could he scrounge some food? It felt like hours since he'd eaten those blueberry muffins. And where were Karen and Tommy? "Too many questions," he sighed.

Leaving the train station, he turned right, following a smooth brick sidewalk into what looked like the downtown area. Maybe he'd get some ideas if he explored the town.

Bobby strolled along nonchalantly, taking in visual details of the place while watching out for trouble. The community was smaller than Coal Town, he noted, but homes and yards were much better cared for. Everything looked perfect — too perfect, really. The colourful houses were freshly painted, and the yards immaculately landscaped. Lawns were weed-free, bushes manicured, and litter was nowhere to be seen. Each driveway had a shiny car or van; some had both!

He passed an older man in a suit carrying a briefcase, a young mother pushing a baby carriage, and two older ladies walking dogs. They didn't speak to him, but nodded or smiled as they passed. He did likewise, not wanting to appear unfriendly and draw attention to himself as an outsider. All had been wearing dressy, fashionable clothing.

"Everybody must be rich here," he thought enviously.

As he approached downtown, orderly signs above store entrances indicated owners' names and business types: several clothing outlets, a grocery chain, a hardware store, some boutiques, and a few restaurants. The town hall and police station shared an impressive red stone building, with majestic elm trees lining the walkway. Brightly painted crosswalks marked each intersection and pedestrians crossed only at these sites, even if no cars were present.

"Wow," Bobby murmured in amazement, "What an orderly place!"

Main Street ended with a stop sign and crossroad bordering a large, open park. On the corner stood a small variety store, simply named *Al's*. It was less imposing than some of the earlier shops, though brightly painted with well-cared-for grounds. Thinking this might be a safe place to gather information, and maybe a snack, Bobby stepped inside.

"Can I help you?" queried the young man standing behind the cash register.

Bobby, nervous about his clothing, answered haltingly, improvising his story. "Well ... maybe you ... could answer some questions," he began. "I arrived in town this morning and my aunt was supposed to meet me at the train station, but she didn't show up." Wearing the new clothing, he had to lie, he reasoned, or admit to being a thief. One dishonesty just led to another.

"Is that right?" replied the storekeeper. "What's her name? I know most people who live here."

Bobby swallowed; he hadn't thought about how small the town was. "I'm not sure of her last name. You see, I never did meet her. She's my grandmother's sister and I just know her as Aunt May," he lied.

"May ..." The man thought for a moment, shaking his head. "Hmm, I don't know anyone named May," he finally said.

"Could be a family nickname," Bobby offered. "Maybe I'll check over at the police station," he added to deflect suspicion. "Do you mind if I look around for a few minutes?"

"Go ahead. If you need help, just holler."

Bobby's legs felt wobbly as he walked down an aisle. All these lies were getting complicated, but no way was he going to poorman's jail. The shelves in *Al's* were similar to corner stores at home, with a good variety of stock. Although the labels and product names were different, Bobby had no trouble finding what he was looking for. Fingering two candy bars, he glimpsed to find the storekeeper absorbed in a magazine. Smoothly, he shoved the bars into his pocket. Then, relying on his practiced technique from home, he picked up two more bars, and approached the counter.

"How much are these, Mister?"

The storekeeper regarded Bobby, then the bars, "Two dollars."

"I don't have that much," Bobby replied. "I think I lost my wallet or left it at home."

The man shrugged his shoulders and tilted his head in a gesture of empathy. Bobby mistook it as pity, something he'd seen too many times. "I didn't really want these anyway," he snapped, dropping the bars on the counter as he turned to leave.

"You can have one if you want," the man offered. "When you find your aunt and get settled in, you can pay me back."

"I don't need charity," retorted Bobby, again misinterpreting the man's kindness. "I'm not poor, you know."

The storekeeper just shook his head as the door slammed.

Outside, Bobby sneered, angry at the perceived ridicule. "I showed him," he muttered, patting his pocket, while diagonally crossing the street to the park. "They all think they're so good here."

Nestled among the sculpted hedges and cultivated trees was a small playground, with benches and tables, slides and swings. Bobby chose a bench under a large maple tree, with a view of the playground area, where a few adults with their small children laughed and played. Starving, he yanked the chocolate bars from his pocket, accidentally dislodging the compass in his haste. Retrieving it from the grass, he noticed the arrow had once again moved, now pointing directly at the L.

"Maybe it's broke," he guessed, stuffing it back in his pocket.

Ripping open his spoils, he devoured the bars, barely registering their smooth, chocolaty taste. If his mom ever found out about this, the clothes or all the lies, he'd be in big trouble. But what else could he have done?

"They're all rich, anyway," he rationalized.

Spotting a water fountain by the swings, Bobby hastily tossed his wrappers to the ground and headed over for a much-needed drink. While quenching his thirst, he heard footsteps and voices approaching.

Two men and a young boy, clad in fancy tracksuits and expensive sneakers, were advancing purposefully in his direction.

"There he is," the boy cried, pointing at Bobby. "He littered; I saw him."

"Okay, William, you stay here," ordered the short, stocky man in front.

"Yeah, son, we'll handle this!" assured the second man, taller, thinner and sporting a moustache.

"He must be a vagrant."

"Yeah, nobody from Rail Town ever litters."

Bobby began backing away.

"He belongs in the poorman's jail."

"Well, we should give him an escort, eh?"

A few paces behind, the wide-eyed-boy blurted, "Is he a crook, Dad?"

"Don't you worry, son, he won't be here long," his father promised. "We're taking him to the police station."

Back-pedaling, Bobby had to sidestep a hedge to keep from falling. This was getting really weird. "What's the matter with you?" he shouted, concentrating on the red-faced short guy. "I didn't do anything to you ... I'll pick up the wrappers, okay?"

"We don't want your kind in our town," the man retorted, jabbing a stubby finger in Bobby's face. "You're coming with us to the police."

Bobby was scared. The police might find out about the bars, and lies, and clothes. "Oh, no I'm not," he snarled, bolting away. "You're all crazy! Leave me alone!"

However, flight was futile. The men caught hold of his arms within seconds, pulling him to a stop. Bobby struggled in terror but was easily restrained by his bigger, stronger captors.

"What's wrong with you?" he protested as they half carried, half pushed him toward the police station. "I didn't do anything!"

Inside the station, behind a counter filled with vases of flowers, loomed a burly, overweight man. His uniform, badge, and holstered gun confirmed his status. To his right were bars and an empty cell.

"What's up, George?" the officer asked the taller man holding Bobby.

"Officer Backstrom, Henry and I caught this boy littering in the park, and it was on purpose. We have a witness," he added, gesturing to his son, William, who was peeking in the doorway.

"And I saw him jaywalk, too," offered William, feeling important.

The big policeman glared at Bobby.

"There were no signs," Bobby cried, his voice shaking.

"See, he doesn't belong here," stated George. "He should be in poorman's jail."

"I'm *not* poor!" Bobby replied angrily.

Passing through a swinging gate, the officer took Bobby's arm from the men. "We'd better talk to the mayor," he cautioned. "He is only a minor."

"I'm no miner," Bobby replied, "I'm too young."

The big man smiled, explaining as they walked, "A minor is a young person, under the age of sixteen." Bobby didn't answer, but his cheeks coloured.

The mayor's office was on the second floor of the Town Hall. His door was always open, so the group hushed respectfully as they topped the stairs leading to the entrance. Tommy dragged his feet sullenly; unhappy and worried about the situation he'd created. Officer Backstrom knocked on the doorjamb.

Looking up from paper work, the mayor's eyes took in the approaching group. After receiving a brief nod of permission, Officer Backstrom, with Bobby in tow, moved toward the big oak desk.

"Excuse us, Your Honour," he began. "These good citizens observed this boy," he indicated Bobby, "purposefully littering and jaywalking. They believe him to be a vagrant, undesirable for our community and a candidate for poorman's jail."

George, Henry and William earnestly nodded their agreement.

"Is that so?" replied the white-haired mayor, moving forward from his seat.

Bobby, with clenched teeth, fighting tears, glared at the advancing figure. His defiance melted, however, when kind blue eyes locked his gaze.

"You can leave the boy with me," said the mayor softly. "I'll take care of things."

Nobody questioned him. They uttered parting words of thanks, with Officer Backstrom pulling the door closed behind them.

"What's your name, young man?" probed the mayor gently, settling once again behind his desk.

"Bobby," was the whispered reply.

"Well, Bobby, sit down and let's discuss things." He indicated a chair beside the desk.

"I didn't know I did anything wrong, Your Honour," Bobby blurted, tears finally rimming his eyes.

"Call me Gus," replied the mayor, pushing back his snowy bangs. "It's adults who like using those honorific titles." He paused, consulting some papers on his desk for a moment, then asked, "Are you poor, Bobby?"

"No!" said Bobby emphatically. "How come everybody asks me that?"

Blueberries and Coal & Inside the Triangle   **49**

"What does poor mean to you?" Gus queried his voice soft and reassuring.

"Not having any money or nice clothes or stuff like that," Bobby replied.

"Lack of possessions, in itself, doesn't make a person poor," explained the mayor. "Poverty in attitude is much more serious. When a person doesn't respect himself or others, he truly is poor. Lying, stealing, greediness, vandalism, bullying, rudeness—the list goes on—all give him away. If he measures his life only by what he lacks, or others possess, *that's* poverty."

Bobby stared at the floor.

"It's not so much the outer wealth as the inner that determines a rich life," Gus continued. "Understand?"

He gently lifted the boy's chin. "So … are you poor?"

Bobby, finally understanding, burst into tears. Gentle arms cradled him, giving comfort. "Self-respect and honesty are your means to riches," Gus whispered. "It truly is your own choice."

Strangely, Bobby wasn't embarrassed by his emotional outburst in front of Gus. The mayor was different … someone to trust … not someone to lie to. Sniffling, he shifted position, the compass falling from his pocket. Gus retrieved it without comment, placing it face up on his desk, the arrow still pointing directly toward the L.

After a few deep breaths, a decision made, Bobby looked up. "I'm going to tell you the truth, sir, all of it."

Tentatively at first, he began his story, talking about his hometown and his jealousy of others. As he spoke, he felt better, somehow cleaner. Words came easier as details of his stealing, the cave-in, and the events in Rail Town were revealed.

Unnoticed by Bobby, the compass arrow edged slowly to the left, closer to the H, as he talked.

NINE

"Wow, your building is so tall," marvelled Karen, straining her neck skyward.

"It is," laughed Gus. "And we're going to the top, the 25th floor," he added, enjoying her wonder.

"The penthouse …."

"Yep," he answered, tugging her toward the entrance.

Still looking upward, Karen stumbled on the first step. "I've never seen a high-rise before."

"Well, this building is small compared to some in the downtown area," said Gus, again steering her toward the door.

Inside, plants, trees, and wrought iron benches lined the mirrored walls of the lobby. Karen's head swiveled left and right as she and Gus approached the elevator doors. "It's beautiful," she whispered. Gus just smiled as he directed her inside the elevator. He then inserted and twisted his key that allowed access to the penthouse level.

Karen clutched her stomach during the fast upward ride, feeling a bit queasy. Ever observant, Gus talked in monologue, trying to distract her. "Mabel and I retired here a few years ago," he said, "and we were lucky enough to get a top-floor apartment. Each penthouse unit has a small outdoor area where grass and shrubs can be planted, giving us our own little patch of nature."

The elevator stopped smoothly, the open doors revealing a long, carpeted hallway brightened by overhead skylights. Gus interrupted his one-sided conversation at the third door, knocking in an odd rhythm. "It's our secret code," he whispered. "You have to be careful in a big city."

His wife, smiling widely, opened the door. "Hello, handsome, you're right on time."

Karen hid behind Gus, embarrassed by her dirty clothes and coal-smudged face.

"Oh, you have company," Mabel exclaimed, mildly surprised. "Well," she invited, addressing Karen, "do come in."

Their apartment was cozy, with colourful paintings, knickknacks, and plants adding to its warmth. While Karen waited in the dining room, perched on a wooden chair that wouldn't stain, Gus and Mabel talked privately in the kitchen.

The older woman wasn't what Karen had expected. True, she was small in height like her husband and she had the same white hair and kind manner, but surprisingly, given the conversation en route, she was overweight — quite notably. Her face was round and cheerful, her whole appearance glowing with health.

"Now, Gus, you know I'm not the one to ask weight questions," voiced Mabel, no longer whispering. "Just about everyone in this city has a weight issue."

Curiously, Karen gazed toward the kitchen, very interested in the dialogue.

"People are obsessed with thinness and they all look sick, if you ask me!" Mabel finished.

"Yes, dear, I know how you feel, and you know I agree," Gus soothed, peeking into the dining room to Karen's watchful gaze. He winked, and raised his index finger to indicate a few more moments, then whispered something close to his wife's ear. Mabel nodded, murmured a reply, then side by side, smiling genuinely, they returned to the dining room.

"Karen," started Gus, "my wife, Mabel."

Standing, Karen took Mabel's hand in a brief greeting. "Pleased to meet you, ma'am ... um ... you'll have to excuse my appearance," she flustered, indicating her stained jeans and dirty hands.

"Nonsense," replied Mabel reassuringly. "Gus told me what happened. The first thing you need, young lady, is a shower and some fresh clothes," she continued. "I may have some old clothes that will fit you; I wasn't always this heavy," she added without a trace of regret or concern.

"I can't believe this is happening," Karen thought, placing a pair of yellow silk pajamas on the vanity and hanging a white terry cloth robe on the door hook. Compared to home, even the bathroom was luxurious, and everything sparkled. "Except me," she murmured, grimacing at her mirror image above the sink.

As she removed her jeans, Karen remembered the signal mirror in her back pocket. Twirling the silver handle, she admired the fancy scrollwork around its perimeter. "Strange there's no dirt on this," she mused, tilting it to check her reflection.

She gasped! Her face was dirty but her cheeks looked puffy, her chin a lot rounder than she remembered. "Oh my gosh," she exclaimed, almost dropping the silver mirror in shock, "I am FAT!"

Reflexively, she turned to the vanity, relieved to see her usual image, not the obese Karen in the hand mirror. "There's something wrong with this thing," she muttered, chancing a second look in the small lens. She tilted the glass to reflect her trunk and abdomen, again gasping in horror. Her belly

Blueberries and Coal & Inside the Triangle   53

was sticking out, fat rolls hanging obscenely over the elastic of her panties. Stretch marks pocked her stomach and grossly swollen thighs.

Moaning, she dropped the mirror on the sink counter and slumped to the floor. "It's just the mirror," she whispered. "It can't be true!" Slowing her breathing, she rubbed her thighs, then her stomach, reassuring herself that the distorted image was false. Cautiously, she pulled herself up to confront the vanity.

Relief coursed through her. Her face was thin and she could count ribs on her bony chest. She climbed on the counter to see her abdomen and legs, turning in all directions. The fat rolls were gone, but Karen still didn't like the way her lower belly seemed to stick out. Her legs were as always, not fat at all. Finally reassured, she climbed back down.

Carefully, Karen covered the hand mirror with a towel, unwilling to chance further lies. "Must be a trick mirror," she reasoned, getting into the shower. "Maybe I'll show it to Mabel."

She took a long, refreshing shower, luxuriating in the warm water, perfumed soap and shampoo. Her fingertips were all wrinkled when she finally turned off the water and dried herself with a thick bath towel. Everything was so unreal.

Mabel's pajamas, though a little big, felt wonderful to Karen after the grime of her old clothes, and the robe was perfect. Glimpsing herself in the vanity and reassured by her usual, now clean reflection, Karen pondered the hand mirror. "It's sick … and mean." She shivered, remembering the rolls of fat. Spooked, she stuffed the lens into a pocket and reached for the door.

In the kitchen, Mabel was preparing a plate of chickpea salad sandwiches, anticipating Karen's hunger. Hearing the bedroom door open, she turned to see Karen in the hallway, carrying her old clothes.

"Why don't I throw those in the washer while we eat some lunch?" Mable queried, taking Karen's dirty bundle.

"Are you sure?"

"Yes, I am. Now you go sit with Gus in the living room and relax," Mabel ordered, gesturing cheerfully. "I'll have everything ready in a few minutes."

Gus and Mabel were easy to like and Karen felt comfortable in their home. During the meal, her hosts maintained an easy banter, describing the city and some of its customs.

When the discussion turned to thinness, Mabel spoke with conviction: "It's not right. Almost everybody in this city is malnourished. There's too much social pressure. Magazines, billboards, television ... *To be in, be thin* ... *Thinning is winning* ... *Fat's not where it's at!* Slogans are everywhere," she continued, obviously frustrated. "Our educators must do a better job of teaching people to respect their bodies and their health."

"Mabel used to be a high-school teacher," explained Gus. "She saw first-hand how a number of her students got caught up in this thinness craze. Several ended up in hospital, and a few actually died of bulimia and starvation. Experiences like that change a person," he continued. "She's very passionate about protecting kids."

"What do you think about all this, Karen?" asked Mabel.

"Well, I haven't been here long enough to really know," Karen replied evasively.

"No, I don't mean this city. I mean you," Mabel probed.

Karen paused, uncomfortable with the question. "I think weight is personal," she replied, examining the tabletop as she spoke. "We all want to be accepted and pleased with our appearance."

"Exactly," interjected Mabel, "but what determines our cultural ideal of body size?" Without waiting for an answer, she

Blueberries and Coal & Inside the Triangle **55**

continued passionately, "Advertising and fashion, that's what!" She slammed her fist against the table. "It's greedy designers preying on impressionable adolescents …."

"Mabel," interrupted Gus, "your blood pressure."

"Oh, you …."

Laughing, Gus resumed, "Personally, I think mirrors should be banned."

Gus's remark reminded Karen. Retrieving the hand mirror from her robe pocket, she held it up for the couple to see. "I found this in that mine I told you about, just after the cave-in. This is a weird mirror though, maybe a trick one. When I look in it, I … I'm … really FAT!" She shuddered.

"Let me see," said Gus, taking the mirror. He examined the handle and scroll work appreciatively, before regarding his reflection. "All I see is my usual good-looking self," he joked, smiling. "Here, Mabel, what do you think?"

Mabel peered at her image and shook her head. "I look like a well-fed, happy old woman," she laughed. Angling the mirror toward Gus, she chuckled, "You handsome devil." Then Karen. "Oh, you *do* look different!" she gasped, passing the mirror back to Gus.

"Your reflection looks about 15 kilograms heavier than you really are, Karen," Gus blurted in a surprised tone. "How odd," he added, his face wrinkled in thought. "What a puzzle …?"

Karen shifted the lens, studying Mabel and Gus, then herself. "It *is* just me who looks different," she agreed.

Wearing borrowed slacks, a blouse, and sandals, Karen followed her hosts out into the afternoon sun. She fidgeted with the blouse, tucking and retucking it at the waist.

"Relax," chided Mabel. "Everything looks so much better on you than it ever did on me."

"Look around you," instructed Gus. "Do you think anybody in this big city notices that your blouse is a size too big?"

The noisy streets, filled with interesting shops, traffic, and people quickly distracted Karen from her self-absorption. Gus was right, she realized; passersby rarely even glanced at her as they bustled about.

"Stay close, Karen," Mabel warned, grasping her elbow. "Rush hour gets hectic!"

Mesmerized by the sights, Karen merely nodded, passively allowing Mabel to direct her through traffic, both following Gus's lead. The older couple rarely journeyed out during rush hour, and never to this section of the city. However, this was not a casual tour; Mabel had a purpose.

Waiting for the traffic light to change, Karen spotted a brightly lit restaurant, the *Exercise Café*. "What's that about?" she asked innocently.

"That's a restaurant where anorexics hang out," answered Gus, leading her and Mabel to the entrance. "They have a low-calorie meal, and then work out on walking machines or exercise bikes." He held the door open. "Come have a look."

The cafe was divided into two sections, one with tables where a few people were eating, the other an exercise area. Pictures and posters on the walls showed 'athletes' participating in various exercises and sports. All were extremely thin and bony, looking gaunt and wasted to the observing teen.

"I don't think I want to stay here," Karen stated, disturbed by the skeletal images.

"Come on over to the *Bulimic Club*," suggested Mabel, pointing across the street.

"The what?" asked Karen, suspiciously.

"The *Bulimic Club*," Gus answered.

"As you know, Karen," Mabel explained, "people try and control weight any number of ways. Some calorie-restrict, others diet and exercise, and then there's the bingers and gaggers."

"That last group is the bulimics," interjected Gus.

The club had an odd layout, a semi-circular counter with stools at one end and several tables at the other. In the middle was a large stainless steel circular vat, with a continuous supply of swirling water and a central drain.

"What's that?" asked Karen, indicating the round structure.

"Just watch," whispered Mabel.

As if on cue, a very thin young lady at the counter stood up, pushed her empty plate forward and walked toward the container. Karen was shocked as the woman gagged herself and vomited into the large vat. The sounds and sight made her stomach queasy. None of the other patrons seemed upset though. Indeed, moments later, several other diners moved toward the gurgling container, their intent clear.

"Let's go," whispered Gus, taking Karen's arm and leading her through the exit.

"That's a disgusting place!" huffed Karen, gulping the fresh air.

"Those clubs are scattered all over the city," responded Mabel. "Did you notice the first-aid station at the end of the counter?"

Karen shook her head, still sickened by what she had witnessed.

"Every now and again someone tears a food tube and vomits blood, or faints from gagging, or just passes out from weakness," said Mabel sadly. "While the club caters to bulimics, management wants no deaths, so ambulance technicians are always available."

"Nice of them," Karen muttered sarcastically.

"Hey," interrupted Gus, pointing to a poster tacked to the side of a streetlight, "there's a beauty contest going on at the city gym." He looked at Karen. "Do you want to go?"

"I think I've seen enough," protested Karen in a soft, tired voice. "I don't really care for your city," she added, leaning against a wall for support.

"See what happens when people lose control, Karen?" queried Gus. "Something abnormal seems desirable, no matter the danger."

Mabel put her arm around Karen's shoulders and rested against the wall beside her. "It's not like this everywhere in the city, Karen," she whispered. "Gus and I chose to show you the worst to help open your eyes."

Trembling, tears brimming, Karen stared at the ground.

"You see, Gus told me how sensitive you seemed about your weight," continued Mabel gently.

Karen started to sob, her body shuddering within Mabel's comforting hug. "I wanted to lose weight ... then I got scared I'd put it all back on when I *did* lose it," she stammered. "I'd get so hungry I'd stuff myself ... then feel so full I'd make myself vomit. I never thought it could result in such ... such ... ."

"Sickness," finished Mabel. "I saw it with my students, Karen, an endless battle for the perfect body. No matter how thin, they still felt fat."

"And, I couldn't tell anyone."

"Oh, yes, Karen," soothed Gus, standing close. "That's a big part of the problem—guilt leads to lying and sneakiness."

"And loneliness," Mabel added.

Karen shivered. "I never want to get like *them,*" she vowed, looking toward the *Bulimic Cafe.*

"You don't have to," replied Mabel. "It just takes some knowledge about nutrition, lots of willpower and some support."

"Every journey starts with the first step," encouraged Gus, gently squeezing Karen's hand.

She smiled weakly.

"Well, let's not waste any more time in *this* section of town," huffed Mabel, guiding Karen back onto the sidewalk. "We have some better sights to see and fun things to do."

Blueberries and Coal & Inside the Triangle   59

For the next few hours, Karen had a tremendous time, being whisked around nicer sections of the city by her hosts. They window-shopped, rode a trolley car, went up and down escalators and explored a huge shopping mall. Finally, grumbling with hunger, Gus guided them toward a traditional restaurant. "My treat, ladies," he insisted. "Let's have a feast!"

"He'll do anything to get out of doing dishes," teased Mabel.

Karen had never been in such a fancy restaurant. A pianist played background music; the linen, candles and cutlery enthralled her. She ordered nut loaf with miso gravy, a side order of garlic roasted potatoes and a small garden salad. Gus and Mabel selected Italian pasta dishes. They all had hot apple pie with a large scoop of soy ice cream for dessert.

The meal was heavenly but, by the time she'd finished, Karen felt uncomfortably full. It had been a long time since she'd eaten so much at one sitting. While Gus and Mabel were sipping coffee, she excused herself, heading to the washroom.

Inside, Karen checked every stall, to make sure she was alone. Choosing the one furthest from the door, she stared into the toilet bowl, guiltily debating with herself. Memories of the *Exercise Café* and the *Bulimic Club* swirled, rekindling her revulsion and fear. After several silent minutes of intense struggle, she took a deep breath and turned away.

Mabel was standing behind her, arms wide open, "You made the right choice, Karen. Good for you!"

Ten

For a few more hours, Tommy wandered the circus grounds, trying rides, and eating cotton candy and popcorn. His heart wasn't in it, though; the magic was gone. Empty rides, mechanical laughter, and repetitive music couldn't replace people, and junk food wasn't satisfying his hunger. He was lonely and he wanted to go home.

"Maybe I should'a listened," he mused, thinking about Gus. "Runnin' away didn't help."

Reluctantly, hands stuffed in his pockets, he ambled toward the food court, still wrestling with his pride. "If I gotta work to get outta here, I guess I'll do it," he muttered, spying the table where he'd first met the stubborn old man. He grabbed the bell and shook it vigorously, impatient now that his mind was set.

Moments later, shuffling footsteps heralded Gus's arrival.

"Hi, Tommy," smiled Gus warmly. "What can I do for you?"

"I'm hungry," Tommy replied contritely. "If you know of any work I can do to earn a meal, I'll try to do it." He couldn't look Gus in the eyes for fear of tears.

"I think you're making a good decision, Tommy," answered Gus gently. "Come with me. I do have a job for you." He led Tommy down a small corridor between two food outlets, to a closet filled with cleaning supplies. "The tables, chairs, and counters all need to be wiped. Think you can manage that?"

"I'll do my best," promised Tommy determined to do whatever it took. "Then can I pick out a real meal?"

The next two hours passed quickly as Tommy cleaned and polished the counters, tables, and chairs. Finally finished, he counted five food outlets, four tables, and twenty-four chairs! "Too bad reading isn't as easy as numbers," he thought, carrying his supplies back to the storage room.

An appreciative whistle signaled Gus's return. "The place looks great, Tommy."

Tommy beamed at the unexpected praise. He had worked hard and felt kind of proud of his efforts. "Yeah," he agreed, "thanks." Pushing his bangs from his eyes, he added, "Now, how 'bout some real food?"

True to his word, Gus prepared Tommy's order, then sat and conversed with the boy while he ate. A small veggie pizza, large glass of ice water, and a heaping bowl of chile rice chips disappeared in minutes.

"Hard work is worth it, hey?" Gus commented. "Not only did you earn a meal, you did a big job, all by yourself."

"Yeah, but most of the time if I do work, I don't get paid," Tommy replied between bites.

"True, but when it's well done, or it helps someone, don't you feel good inside?"

Tommy thought about that while sipping his ice water. "But what about when you try, and you can't do it?" he finally offered, remembering his school difficulties. "That doesn't make you feel very good."

"Then," said Gus, looking directly into Tommy's eyes, "you have to be honest with yourself and ask for help. We all find some things easy and others much more difficult. But you shouldn't give up just because you have to try harder."

"You make it sound simple," said Tommy, looking up at the old man. "Can *you* help me to read?"

"Maybe," Gus replied, rubbing his chin. "It depends how hard you want to work. You see, I have a problem, too, and maybe you can help me."

Tommy sat up straight, quickly understanding what Gus was proposing. "You mean you'll help me if I help you?"

Gus nodded. "That giant tree you saw on your way in is blocking the park exit, so nobody comes here anymore. Got any ideas?"

Eyes glinting, Tommy reached into his back pocket. "Hey," he exclaimed, holding up the chisel, "Maybe I can make a tunnel through the tree with this."

Gus smiled, shaking his head. "It's a pretty thick tree, Tommy; I don't think ...."

"So," interrupted Tommy, "it'll just take some hard work, an' like you said, we can't give up without tryin'."

Gus looked at the boy, his clear blue eyes twinkling.

"I saw a hammer over at the bell-ringing place; you know, where people try to be a strongman," Tommy continued, walking in circles as he made his plans. "I could use that."

"All right, Tommy, you can try," Gus stated good-naturedly. "For every hour you work on that tree, I'll spend an hour teaching you to read. But I think that strongman hammer is too big. Why don't you look in the cleaning supply cupboard first? I'm pretty sure there's a rubber mallet hammer in there."

The pair shook hands to seal the deal, then Tommy practically flew to the storage room to search for the hammer. A small tunnel in that big tree would mean a way home!

Blueberries and Coal & Inside the Triangle   **63**

Tommy was up by dawn from his makeshift bed in the drying room near the park entrance. Thick, fluffy towels made a comfortable mattress but even so, he'd had a restless sleep. At first, memories of his family kept him awake. When he finally did fall asleep, all he'd dreamt about was that monster tree and the tunnel.

After his meal last evening, it was too dark outside to start his project. Besides, the day had been a very long one and he'd been pretty tired. It was Gus who'd suggested that the drying room might make a good place to bunk for the night. Now, he was anxious to get started, he wanted to get home.

Carrying his chisel and mallet, he approached the giant redwood, awed by its size and majesty. Surveying the trunk for a starting point, Tommy silently apologized for what he had to do. "I gotta get home," he whispered. A gentle breeze rustling high up among the upper branches swayed the sequoia back and forth, as if granting permission.

The knobby bark was rough to his touch, but Tommy had no trouble breaking its surface. His rubber mallet, no bigger than a carpenter's hammer, was light and easy to use. And the chisel … well, it was amazing! Whether the little blade was very sharp, the wood in the tree very soft or a combination of both, the tunnel grew quickly.

In his first hour, Tommy cut a half-metre circle, almost a fifty centimetres deep, into the tree. After the second, he'd carved out another seventy centimetres before finding it too narrow to properly swing the hammer.

Frustrated, Tommy retreated, standing amidst the growing pile of wood chips. His arms ached all the way up to his shoulders and blisters were starting on both hands. "This is hard work," he muttered, wiping sweat from his forehead. "But, I'm gonna get outta here."

Needing more space, he chiseled an outline of a larger circle around the tunnel, doubling its size. Then, aside from a few water breaks, he worked four straight hours, reaching halfway through the trunk.

It was almost noon when Gus arrived. "Amazing!" he shouted, both pleased and surprised at Tommy's progress. "How on earth did you get so much done? You must have gotten up very early."

"Motivation, Gus," Tommy retorted, grinning at the praise.

"That must be a good blade you have there."

Proudly, Tommy passed his tool to Gus, valuing the older man's opinion. Gus noticed the boy's palms. "Oh, Tommy," he murmured, "you've got some nasty blisters." Pocketing the chisel, Gus gently grasped Tommy's hands. "Let me have a look."

Tommy's hands were so stiff he could hardly open them. Broken blisters, crusted with blood, riddled most fingers and both palms.

"I have some salve that will help, Tommy," Gus said sympathetically. "You can put it on while we practice some reading."

"Guess I should'a wore gloves," Tommy winced, his palms burning.

"I'll rummage up a pair for later," promised Gus, retrieving the chisel. "Whew," he whistled, marveling at the instrument's fine workmanship. "This is a beautiful tool. Just look at this edge ... and the calligraphy!"

"Did you see the letters?" asked Tommy innocently.

"That's what calligraphy is, Tommy," explained Gus patiently, "beautifully formed writing."

"Oh," Tommy nodded, repeating the new term. "I can't understand them, though."

"Do you know any of the letters?"

Tommy looked closely at the blade. "M, no W, O, O, D, C, H, I, S, E, L, C, U, T, S, W or M, O, O, D, L, I, K, E, B, U, T, T, E, R."

Blueberries and Coal & Inside the Triangle   65

"Very good, Tommy. You got them all. Try to remember, a space between the letters means the end of one word and the beginning of another." Gus drew the first four letters on the ground using the chisel. "Do you know how to sound out words?"

Tommy shook his head, but didn't feel embarrassed with Gus. The white-haired man settled beside the boy on the ground, and demonstrated the sounds of each letter. Tommy listened intently, concentrating on every detail. "So, when the letter o is doubled," Gus explained, "it doesn't have a long 'o' sound, or a short 'au' sound, it sounds like the 'oo' in boo, or the 'ou' in could."

Tommy grouped the first four letters, sounding them out, "Wwwooood. Wwoood. Wood. Wood!"

"Right!" cried Gus with enthusiasm. "Come on. Let's go back to the food court and fix your hands. Then I'll get us something to eat while you look at some books I found for you."

Tommy wiggled his nose at the strong smell of the salve. "You sure about this?" he queried, but Gus was already busy in the kitchen. Haltingly, Tommy slopped a glob on his palms. It didn't sting, so he began massaging it over both hands. Almost immediately, coolness eased the aching and stiffness.

"This stuff is great," he exclaimed, wiggling his fingers.

While Gus prepared the meal, Tommy leafed through books piled on the food court table. The early grade readers with simple words gave meaning to common pictures. He carefully examined the letters, tracing them with his fingers. Never had he put so much effort into schoolwork. Using visual clues from pictures and the little he knew about sounding out, he was soon deciphering simple letter combinations like "tree" and "water". Concentrating deeply on his task, he was startled when Gus called him to his meal.

"You're working hard, Tommy," commented Gus.

The boy nodded, hungrily eyeing his lentil burger, curly fries, coleslaw, and chocolate soy milk. "Thanks, Gus," he said appreciatively. Pointing to his glass, "That was in one of the books…M, I, L, K — milk," he added proudly. Gus smiled and patted Tommy on the back.

"See what you can do when you really concentrate? Now, what does glass start with?"

"Glass … guh … guh … gee. It starts with G!"

The rest of the meal was spent practicing letter sounds. Tommy had never known learning could be so much fun. Best of all, Gus didn't laugh if mistakes occurred; he'd just tell Tommy to rethink his answer and try again. It was Tommy who laughed when he mixed something up.

Together, the young boy and older man worked and laughed, as the hours ticked by.

Eleven

"First step — get rid of these clothes," sighed Bobby, once again in the train station washroom. Emptying the garment bag of his own clothing and footwear, he grimaced at their filth.

"I don't know how Dad stands this," he murmured.

Once changed, he felt better inside but looked a lot worse outside. His blackened t-shirt, jeans and sneakers badly needed washing. Purposefully, Bobby carried the garment bag, now containing the "borrowed" clothes, to the sour-faced ticket agent.

"Somebody must've forgot these," he said loudly, getting the man's attention. "I found them in the men's washroom."

The sandy-haired man examined the boy and smirked at Bobby's dirty old clothes. Bobby wasn't bothered.

"Clothes don't make the person," he told himself, remembering Gus's words.

Placing the garment bag on the counter, he turned to leave. Unsmiling, the clerk pulled the bag inside and opened the zipper to examine the contents.

"Next step, the corner store," Bobby thought, summoning his courage. As he neared the station door, the station clerk hollered behind him; leaning through the wicket window, he was gesturing Bobby to return. "Hey, you. Come back here!"

"Oh, no," worried Bobby, "I must be in trouble." Fighting an urge to run, he forced his unwilling feet back to the ticket window. Surprisingly, the man didn't look upset; in fact, he was smiling.

"There's a reward offered for these clothes," he informed Bobby. "The person who left them called this morning and had this envelope delivered."

Noting the man's obvious change in attitude, Bobby accepted the packet, his hand shaking a little. "Gus must be right," he thought. "When you carry yourself with pride and honesty, people have to respect that, even if your clothes are grubby."

"Honesty sure does pay," offered the clerk.

Thanking the man, Bobby pocketed his reward, preferring to open the envelope in private. Maybe his luck was changing, he thought, glad he'd acted responsibly. Half a block later, he ripped the envelope open, his curiosity aroused. Inside was a note praising his honesty and a crisp ten-dollar bill!

"Wow, I have money for the train!" he exclaimed.

A few hours ago, he'd probably have purchased the ticket immediately and ignored his other responsibilities, but now, he didn't even consider that. The mayor trusted him to fix his mistakes and Bobby was determined to fulfill his promise. No 'poor man' label for him!

Bobby folded the ten-dollar bill into his pocket, smiling at his good fortune. Humming softly, he scrunched the envelope and note into a ball, tossing them into a street-side waste bin. Passersby smiled approvingly at this civic behaviour, adding to Bobby's good mood.

Blueberries and Coal & Inside the Triangle   69

"It's not just about me," he said, reaching a new understanding. "These people all share in taking care of their town."

As he neared *Al's*, Bobby's confidence sagged and butterflies fluttered in his stomach. Knowing what was right didn't make it easy. He took a big breath and entered the open door.

The same brown-haired young man was behind the counter.

"Hello, mister," began Bobby nervously.

"Hi, there," replied the storekeeper. "Did you find your aunt?"

Bobby swallowed, "Well, sir, that's why I'm here. I have a confession to make. When I was in here earlier," he stammered, "I … I lied." His mouth felt dry and his heart pounded, but he forced himself to meet the young man's steady, blue-eyed gaze. Gradually, gaining confidence as he spoke, Bobby told the true story of how he came to Rail Town.

"… and when I woke up, I was here, and I was filthy." He looked down at his dirty old clothes. "I found some new clothes in the washroom at the train station and took them because I didn't want to get put in poorman's jail. A woman told me that's where they put people who look like me. See, I couldn't tell you the truth about how I got here without telling you I stole those clothes."

"That explains why I didn't know who your 'Aunt May' was," the man recalled. "What happened to those clothes?"

"I brought them back before I came here and gave them to the ticket agent."

"Did you come here to tell me that?"

"Yes, sir, but there's more; I stole two chocolate bars from your store. I was hungry and didn't have any money and didn't want you to think I was poor."

The young man wrinkled his brow, but remained silent.

"But that's no excuse," continued Bobby. "I shouldn't have done it and I shouldn't have lied, either."

"Why did you come back?"

"I'd like to apologize and make amends, if you'll let me. Is there any work you need done?" Bobby stood straight, regarding the young storekeeper expectantly.

"What's your name?" the man asked.

"Bobby."

"I'm Bill," he offered, extending his hand. "I admire your honesty and courage," he continued when Bobby shook his hand tightly. "Now, I could say just forget it, but I think I'll take you up on your offer." He led the boy over to the large display window. "This picture window needs washing, and the floor needs to be swept."

Though they didn't take long, completing the small jobs helped Bobby soothe his guilty conscience. In truth, the payback was probably of more benefit to him than the storekeeper.

"You know, Bobby," said Bill afterwards, "when I first met you this morning, even with those new clothes, you were poorer than you are now. What happened?"

"I met a very nice gentleman in town who helped me understand that the only person I was *really* fooling was myself."

"The mayor?"

"How'd you know?

"It sounds just like him; he's a very fair and wise man. If he gives you advice, it's worth following."

As he left the store, there was a bounce in Bobby's step that hadn't been present for months. His heart felt lighter, somehow cleaner, and he was proud of himself. "Only one more thing to do," he muttered, heading to the site of his earlier arrest. Sure enough, the empty candy bar wrappers were still on the ground. After carefully placing them in a wastebasket, he sat against a tree, reflecting on his day and his reward.

"Who'd 'a thought?" he marveled pulling the money from his pocket. As the bill came free, so did the compass, bouncing face up on the grass.

The hands had moved again, now pointing almost directly at the "H".

In a flash, Bobby realized what the compass measured. He howled with laughter at its simplicity. "It's a lie meter!" Every time he was dishonest, the arrow moved away from the H (Honest) toward the L (Liar). Ironically, now that he knew its purpose, he didn't need it anymore.

Pocketing his money, he stared at the compass, knowing what tasks remained. "Home," he sighed. "I still got some things to fix at home."

But for now, it was mission accomplished and a promised meal with the mayor.

Twelve

Lying on the guestroom bed, Karen stared at the ceiling, unable to sleep. Images from the *Exercise Café* and the *Bulimic Club* kept running through her mind. Those places were horrible, and too real. She shivered, frightened that she, too, could become like that.

She'd always been a good weight for her height — well, maybe 3 kilograms over, but no more. Weight had never been a concern to her; she was happy with who she was … until … until that day.

Everything changed ten months ago at school, on a Monday afternoon. She'd forgotten a book for an assignment and had gone back inside her homeroom to get it. As she was leaving, she heard boys talking in the hall. One voice she knew well — David Frasier, a really cute guy she liked who sat next to her in French and Math.

"Who are you taking to the Christmas dance, David?" a voice asked.

Karen stayed motionless behind the classroom door, straining to overhear his answer.

"I haven't asked anyone," David replied. "I might not go."

"What about that girl, Karen?" said the first voice, "I see you talking with her a lot in class."

Karen almost stopped breathing.

"She's nice," said David softly, "but she's not really the dating type."

"Yeah, and she's kind of … roundish, if you know what I mean," that nameless, but unforgettable voice snickered crudely.

"I didn't say that!" retorted David, an edge to his voice. "We're just friends, and I don't want that to change. Come on. Let's get out of here."

Karen slumped to the floor in disbelief, her heart pounding. Is that what people thought of her? Roundish? Fat! She shuddered, tears brimming.

That evening she only picked at her meal, and then spent hours locked in the bathroom, critically appraising every centimetre of her physique. It became a daily ritual, standing before the mirror, turning in all directions, until she came to agree with the VOICE; she *was* fat!

Cutting calories was tough, but Karen did it, managing to lose two kilograms in the first two weeks. She was always hungry, but even if the scale said she was lighter, the mirror didn't; she still felt fat.

One evening when her parents were out, she devoured a dozen cookies and a huge bowl of potato chips. Afterward, she felt so disgusted at her weakness that she intentionally vomited, flushing away the calories. Strangely, it was worth it; the food tasted so good after all those days of starvation. Soon, this pattern of binging and purging began repeating itself, over, and over, and over.

Karen continued to lose weight, almost 10 kilograms in five months, but no one at home said much. The pit had shut down and her dad was laid off, deflecting both parents' attention from what was happening in *her* life. Besides, the loose sweaters she liked wearing camouflaged her shrinking figure admirably.

In early July, just after her father had gone out west looking for work, Karen got a little careless. Two or three times her mom noticed food particles in the toilet bowl and questioned her about them. Naturally, Karen had to lie, convincingly attributing everything to the flu.

"I don't know, Karen," her mom fretted. "You're too thin. Maybe you should see the doctor."

"Ma, yer just a worry wart," she'd assured. "Nothin's wrong."

Girls at school also noticed her change in size. Some, with their own image problems, thought she looked better—more chic, and quizzed her about her diet. She learned all kinds of tricks from them, like how exercise, laxatives, and just drinking extra water could be used to lose weight.

Not everyone at school thought her weight loss a good thing. Karen smiled, recalling a conversation with David near the end of ninth grade.

"Karen, are you all right?" he asked anxiously. "I ... I mean ... have you been sick?"

"No, I'm fine. Why?"

"Well, you're looking kind of ... thin," he added, concern evident in his voice.

She felt almost vindicated by his words.

"Well, that's the look boys like, isn't it?" she retorted coolly, remembering the overheard conversation.

David looked like a scolded puppy, turning away without further comment. Seeing his hurt, Karen almost apologized for her rudeness. Almost. Though David hadn't voiced the words on that unforgettable day, he hadn't denied them either. She let him walk away.

In a perverse way, Karen liked the increased attention she received. Yet, the more people noticed her thinness, the less

Blueberries and Coal & Inside the Triangle   **75**

satisfied she became with her size. It was a dangerous spiral with a point of no return.

She shuddered, visualizing those skeletal bodies in the downtown restaurants.

"Mabel is right," she thought. "I do deserve better. Calories and body size don't make a life; I want more."

Impulsively, she flipped on her bedside lamp and grabbed the pocket mirror, angling it to see her reflection. "Oohh!" she gasped, sitting up in surprise. Her face looked healthier, still puffy, but the really obese look was gone! Excited, she jumped to her feet, scouring the rest of her body with the small glass. The rolls of fat were a lot smaller and the skin markings harder to see. Everywhere looked better, much better ....

"This mirror shows what you think ... not the reality," she exclaimed with sudden understanding. "That's why my image is fat!"

Thrilled, she hurried to the washroom vanity, seeking confirmation. She flipped back and forth between the large and small mirrors, comparing her reflections. The vanity Karen was the same as usual, smaller, and thinner than the pocket mirror image, but the difference between the two was less than earlier in the day.

"It really is mindset," Karen thought with relief, "just like Mabel and Gus said."

Quietly she returned to bed, promising change. "Healthy food, healthy living, healthy me," she whispered, resolving never to look like the people of this city. "But I'll need help," she admitted, remembering Gus's advice: "Find an ally, a friend you can talk to and trust. You'll need support through the rough times or you might weaken."

"Sounds good," Karen whispered aloud as she snuggled under her covers, "but how do I know the person will be there when I need them?"

She yawned, exhausted from her long day.

"I think I'll talk with Mom and maybe ... David. He seems like a nice person, we get along well, and I really do like him."

Thirteen

The sun was high above the horizon when Tommy emerged from the drying room. "Darn," he exclaimed, heading toward the tree, "I slept in." He twisted and flexed various muscles as he walked, working out the stiffness from yesterday's labours. His palms, surprisingly, looked pretty normal.

Kicking tree shavings away from the opening, Tommy noted the rich smell of freshly cut wood. "Mmmm," he murmured appreciatively, inhaling deeply as he crawled into the tunnel, tools in hand.

"Whaaat?" he exclaimed in surprise, halting abruptly. The tunnel was almost finished!

Hearing footsteps, he backed out, turning to see Gus's smiling face.

"Good morning, Tommy."

"Did you do that?" Tommy demanded, waving his chisel at the tunnel.

"I did," answered Gus, holding out a pair of work gloves. "After you fell asleep, I borrowed your chisel and worked for a couple of hours."

"Why'd you help?" growled Tommy, his eyes narrowed suspiciously. "This was my project."

Gus smiled at the boy's ferocity. "Well, Tommy," he explained, "It is a very big tree, and having a tunnel helps me, too. So I figured it was only fair that I help."

"But I didn't ask for any."

"True, but a person doesn't always need to ask. The task was big enough to share, and I wanted to show my respect for your efforts."

"I could'a done it myself, you know."

"Oh, I know that, Tommy. You've shown yourself to be a good worker. But your hands were pretty bad last night and I know how much you want to go home."

"Well, thanks … I guess," Tommy murmured reluctantly. Flexing his hands, he added, "They don't feel too bad today. That salve must've helped."

"I'm sure it did, but too much work today wouldn't."

The boy thought for a moment. "Yeh, yer right," he finally admitted, "but I would'a finished."

Laughing, Gus tousled the boy's hair. "I think you've proven what determination can accomplish."

Tommy took the work gloves and carefully put them on. "Well, I'm still determined to read!" he replied emphatically, turning toward the tunnel. "Do I get another lesson before I leave?"

"Absolutely," replied Gus. "When you're finished here, come back to the dining area and we'll go over a few things."

Almost immediately, Tommy's hammer and chisel were rhythmically slicing through the wood. As he worked, he visualized letters of the alphabet, practicing the sounds he remembered. Barely an hour passed before the chisel broke through the outer tree bark. Tommy whooped in triumph as daylight flooded into the darkness.

Blueberries and Coal & Inside the Triangle

Moments later, he was standing outside the circus wall, peering back through the completed tunnel.

"Ha, ha, hah, I did it!" he exclaimed, giddy with pride.

Impulsively, he grabbed the chisel and mallet, reaching above the tunnel entrance. "One more thing to finish," he muttered. Carefully, he carved his own sign in the tree bark — TOMMY — for all future visitors to read.

Back inside the park, Tommy wedged the chisel into the tree bark for Gus, in case he ever wanted to enlarge the tunnel. He took the mallet and gloves back to the closet.

When Tommy emerged from the storage area, Gus was in the middle of the food court, setting up a chalkboard filled with words. "You did it!" Gus exclaimed, smiling broadly. "What a big job, Tommy. Thank you for all your hard work."

Tommy was both pleased and embarrassed by the praise. "Someone told me when you have a job, just set your mind to it and then do it," he teased, eyes twinkling.

"Come have a seat," invited Gus, pulling a chair from a nearby table. "These are common words that you'll see a lot. I want you to memorize them as your lesson." He pointed to the first word: *the* and *THE,* pronouncing it aloud, and sounding the individual letters. Tommy repeated the process.

"You have to know both capital and small letters, Tommy," Gus instructed.

The other words were: *in, no, if, and, you, but, get, go, to, car, exit,* and *park.* Tommy, concentrating intently, did everything Gus requested. Next, he closed his eyes and haltingly spelled the words as Gus said them. Finally, Gus erased the board and Tommy wrote the words Gus called out. Reading seemed so much easier here, as Gus, almost magically made the letters understandable to Tommy. "It's that "D" word again, Tommy," smiled Gus.

"Detention?" Tommy teased, grinning saucily. "No, no wait. Could it be ... determination?"

"Maybe delinquent," Gus retorted, chuckling. "Seriously, Tommy, the trick is to practice, practice, practice, and you'll get really good." Gus checked his wristwatch. "Time for us to go; the train arrives on the hour."

Hand in hand, the boy and his mentor walked to the tunnel, then to the crest of the hill. On the way, Gus quizzed Tommy on phonics, playing fun word games to test him.

"What does grass start with?'

"G."

"Say start, but without the last 't.'" Gus pronounced the 't' sound rather than naming the letter.

Tommy thought carefully before answering. "Sta ... star! Star."

When he deciphered a hard word, they'd both laugh, Gus clapping his hands in delight. Tommy had never realized language and learning could be so much fun.

Near the big red slide, Gus pointed to the sign beside its entrance stairs:

NOTICE: THIS PARK HAS NO EXIT.
ONLY ENTER IF YOU PLAN ON STAYING!

"Hey, I know some of the words now," Tommy exclaimed.

"Let's read it together," suggested Gus. "You read most of it and I'll fill in the words that you haven't learned yet."

"Okay," Tommy agreed. "You first."

"Notice, this," Gus started.

"p ... ark, park" sounded Tommy.

"has" read Gus.

"no ... ex ... it," uttered Tommy. "It does now," he added happily

"Only enter," continued Gus.

Blueberries and Coal & Inside the Triangle　　**81**

"if you," said Tommy.

"plan," read Gus.

"on," voiced Tommy confidently.

"staying," finished Gus.

"NOTICE: THIS PARK HAS NO EXIT. ONLY ENTER IF YOU PLAN ON STAYING," read Tommy proudly.

"We can take this down now since you made that exit."

"Yeah, now maybe you'll get more visitors!" the boy replied earnestly.

When they reached the rail tracks, Gus gestured to a sign lying on the ground:

> REMAIN IN THE CAR
> IF YOU DON'T WANT TO STAY
> BUT GET OUT AND
> THE CAR GOES AWAY

"I kicked it over," Tommy admitted, flushing a little. "I couldn't read it. I was so mad, or scared, or both, I guess."

"Let's try to read it now," suggested Gus, fixing it upright. "Okay?"

Tommy nodded.

"First word," said Gus, "Remain."

"in … the … car … if … you," read Tommy.

"don't want," voiced Gus.

"to", added Tommy.

"stay," read Gus. "Next line."

"B … but, g … get oot,"

"Out," corrected Gus.

"out … and … the … car … go … go," stammered the boy.

"s," finished Gus.

"goes … a … wa … way… away! Tommy crowed triumphantly.

"Now, all of it," directed Gus.

"REMAIN IN THE CAR IF YOU DON'T WANT TO STAY BUT GET OUT AND THE CAR GOES AWAY," recited Tommy.

"Hooray!" shouted the older man, beaming with pride. "You did it!"

"Gus, I'm glad I got out," Tommy blurted when they reached the waiting rail car, "because I got to meet you," he gulped, big tears brimming his eyes and running down his cheeks. "You showed me how to read."

Gus gave Tommy a big hug, patting his back affectionately and helping him into his seat, "I didn't really show you how to read, Tommy; I showed you how to learn. When you get back home, remember two very important things: believe in yourself and be ...?"

"DETERMINED!" they both chorused in unison.

"You may not remember all the lessons we did," Gus soothed, "but, with practice, they'll come back quickly."

"I'll miss you, Gus," Tommy whispered, his eyes getting heavy.

"And I you, young man."

Tommy nodded sleepily as he snuggled into the cushioned seat of *The Help Yourself Rail* car. "I shouldn't be so sleepy," he muttered. "G'bye Gus."

"Good bye, Tommy," the old man answered waving his hand slowly. "Try and remember ...."

"Believe in myself and be determined," Tommy sleepily answered, repeating it over and over, as he drifted into a deep slumber.

Fourteen

En route to the train station, Bobby ambled alongside the older man, trying to match Gus's long, slow strides. Everyone they passed waved, smiled or shouted a greeting to the white-haired mayor, all eager to show respect and friendship.

"Wow, everybody seems to really like you," Bobby observed, amazed at the obvious popularity of his host.

"I like to think it's because they trust me and know I strive for honesty at all times," replied Gus. "But sometimes," he winked, "it's because they want a favour."

As they entered the train station, a silver-haired man wearing a pin-stripe suit waved and gestured to the mayor.

"Excuse me a moment, Bobby," Gus chuckled, his eyes twinkling. "This might be one of those favours." He steered Bobby toward the ticket window. "Why don't you pay for your trip while I talk to this gentleman?"

"Sure, Gus," Bobby agreed. "Take your time."

The clerk, a thin balding man, smiled through his thick beard as Bobby approached. "Where to, young man?" he asked.

"Well, I want to take *The Help Yourself Rail* to Coal Town," answered Bobby. "Do you sell tickets for there?"

"You bet, just ten dollars, no matter where you're going."

Bobby dug in his pocket and pulled out the ten-dollar reward. "Here you go, mister."

"The train will be here in about fifteen minutes," the ticket man informed him. "As long as you stay in the station, you don't need a ticket," he continued, "so let me know if you want a later train and I'll give you one."

"Oh, no," answered Bobby, "I'll be on this one."

To his left, Bobby noted Gus was still engaged in conversation. Waving to catch the older man's attention, he pointed to the loading platform and then exited the station in search of a bench.

The lady he'd met on arrival was sitting on the nearest one, reading a magazine. Bobby grimaced, remembering her rude comments. As he passed, she recognized him and, surprisingly, smiled.

Though his hair, face, and hands were now clean, Bobby's clothing was still coal stained filthy. Puzzled at her change in attitude, he stopped. "Excuse me, ma'am, but I have to ask you something," he began warily.

"Go ahead," the woman replied in a friendly tone.

"Yesterday morning, you weren't very nice to me, sayin' I'd end up in the poorman's jail. Today, you're smilin' at me — friendly like. Why?"

"Well, today your spirit is rich and clear; I see it in your eyes and posture. Yesterday, you were closed, wary, and suspicious. Frankly, your aura wasn't ... honest and you looked rather ... poor ... inside."

"So, poorman's jail is a place you put yourself?" he queried, understanding her point.

"Yes!" she trilled. "See how you've changed!"

Blueberries and Coal & Inside the Triangle

Bobby wandered to an empty bench, reflecting on the woman's words. "Maybe she was right in what she saw yesterday," he stewed, "but she didn't have to be so rude about it!"

A hand on Bobby's shoulder signaled Gus's arrival. "I saw how respectful you were," the older man commented, nodding to the other bench. "You've grown a lot in just a short time," he praised.

"I've learned some good things from you," Bobby replied.

"Maybe so," agreed the mayor, "but not everyone takes advice, or acts on it, like you've done."

Screeching noise heralded the arrival of *The Help Yourself Rail*.

"Right on time," commented Gus.

"For such a small train, it sure makes a lot of noise," complained Bobby, covering his ears playfully.

He pulled the metal compass from his pocket and held it out to the older man. "Gus, I want you to take this — a present — to remember me by." Bobby's voice shook a little, but he withheld tears. "I don't need a compass anymore to tell me right from wrong."

Gus accepted the gift and drew Bobby close in a hug. "Remember, Bobby, you *are* a good person. When you get home, believe in yourself and be truthful, and success will follow."

Not trusting his voice, Bobby just nodded as he climbed into the familiar seat.

"Bye, Bobby," said Gus, waving as the car lurched forward.

"Thanks, Gus," Bobby hollered, twisting around in his seat. "I won't forget you!" he added, waving enthusiastically.

Moments later, Rail Town was no longer visible. Yawning, Bobby curled up in his seat, tired from his recent adventures. Eyes closed, he whispered Gus's advice as sleep claimed him:

"Believe in myself and be truthful; believe in myself and be truthful …."

Fifteen

Throwing back the bedcovers, Karen lifted her arms over her head, stretching to shake off morning cobwebs. Then, sitting on the edge of her bed, she pulled on her old jeans and t-shirt, anticipating her journey home to Coal Town. So much had changed.

Briefly, she toyed with the little hand mirror, sticking her tongue out at her larger-than-life image. "Everyone in this city needs one of these," she thought wryly, picturing the skeletal people she'd seen. Shuddering, she placed the mirror in the top drawer of her night table; Mabel would know someone who could use it.

As she made her way to the washroom, delicious kitchen smells tickled her nostrils. Karen inhaled deeply and smiled, touched that Mabel was preparing her a special breakfast. They were such nice people; it seemed she'd known them forever. The only sad thing about leaving this place would be leaving them.

"Will I ever see you again?" she'd asked last night.

Mabel smiled gently as Gus answered, "We'll always be in your heart ... and your memories."

After a breakfast alive with talk, laughter, and wonderful food, the trio slowly made their way to the subway station, wandering through some of the newer downtown sections. The sights were still surreal to Karen, so different from home. The tall buildings demanded her attention at the expense of her feet.

"You're a precious girl, Karen," chuckled Mabel, grasping her hand after a near fall, "inside and out."

"I do feel better, Mabel," replied Karen seriously. "I ... I'm going to make sure I stay healthy."

"Anytime you feel too heavy or think you need to slim down, just remember people like them," whispered Gus as they passed a group of five or six emaciated teenage girls.

Karen shivered, recognizing that her fate could have been similar. "I will, Gus," she promised.

Lively conversation and sightseeing made the walk enjoyable, though too short in Karen's estimation. She was going to miss these wonderful, caring people.

"After the next subway train, *The Help Yourself Rail* should arrive," predicted Gus as they descended stairs to the subway platform. "It's such a small rail car, I'm afraid you'll have to use that little ladder again," he added, gesturing with his hand.

"That might be hard for us, Gus," said Mabel laughing, "But for this young lady — no trouble."

The trio stopped at the edge of the platform overlooking the tracks, next to the small, metal ladder. Karen looked from Mabel to Gus and back again, as she spoke, trying to keep her voice steady. "I've learned so much in such a short time from you both." Then hugging her two mentors warmly, she whispered her thanks.

Mabel squeezed her affectionately. "Remember, Karen, it's the inner you that keeps your life in perspective."

A loud squealing announced the arrival of *The Help Yourself Rail*. Fighting tears, Karen climbed onto the ladder with Gus steadying her arm. As she descended, Gus reminded her,

"Karen, believe in yourself and be disciplined. If you do that, you'll conquer anything."

Karen, no longer trusting her voice, just nodded her head in agreement.

At the bottom of the ladder, it only took a few steps to reach the little rail car. Tears blurred her vision as she settled into the soft cushioned seat. Mable and Gus watched and waved as she looked up one last time. "I'll miss you," she mouthed, the noises of the subway drowning out her voice.

The car slowly moved forward.

"Believe in myself and be disciplined," she whispered over and over as sleep once again claimed her.

Sixteen

Rose cleared her throat, trying to ignore the camera pointed in her direction. She wasn't used to public speaking, and had never been on television before.

"I have three children," she began, "Karen, fifteen, Bobby, eleven, and Tommy, seven." Her voice shook nervously. "Their dad, Buddy, a miner, is in Alberta—looking for steady work, now that the mine here is closed. The children were bringing home some coal from an old bootleg pit for the stove." She hesitated briefly, shifting her gaze to the red wagon and pit opening. "It looks like the mine caved in …." Her voice broke as tears formed.

Phonse continued the dialogue: "Mrs. MacDonald found the children's shovels and wagon just outside the cave-in entrance last evening. Rescue crews have been arriving here throughout the night and early morning. First reports indicate a vertical drop of over thirty metres. The initial priority of work crews has been to widen the opening and improve air flow to the shaft."

The camera zoomed in on the mine opening and ventilation hosing. "A rescue crew is now preparing to enter the mine — almost sixteen hours after the cave-in is thought to have occurred."

Scanning the crowd, the cameraman brought his lens back to Rose as Phonse continued, "Earlier this morning, a microphone was lowered into the cavern, but no noises or voices have yet been heard. Still, rescue officials profess confidence that the MacDonald children will be found."

Rose had returned home from work around 6:00 p.m. the evening prior, a little later than usual. The house and yard were empty when she arrived. "Where are the kids?" she'd wondered, thinking it a bit odd that none of them were home. However, it was a very nice evening and still very bright out. She just figured they'd be arriving soon.

By the time she'd prepared a big pot of vegetable soup and some peanut butter sandwiches, and still no one arrived home, she was getting worried. Several phone calls later, her anxiety was approaching panic. None of the neighbors had seen her children since early in the day.

Then, she'd remembered. "Fox Farm — they were diggin' coal." She ran out into the backyard to the coal bin. Sure enough the wagon was missing and there was fresh coal on the ground in front of the bin.

"Oh, my God, somethin' must have happened."

A million and one scenarios played out in her mind as she half-walked, half-ran to the rolling, barren area of Fox Farm. Thankfully, summer ensured good visibility late into the evening. It was near 8:30 p.m. when Rose, frantic with worry, reached the blueberry-filled hills, her breathing ragged. She searched and called their names, over and over as she moved deeper and deeper into the shadow-filled landscape. Her children were nowhere to be seen.

Then, finally as she'd scanned the fields and hills to the east, sunlight glinted off something red. After racing to the spot,

Blueberries and Coal & Inside the Triangle   91

Rose found Tommy's battered old wagon and some digging tools lying on the ground. Just beyond the wagon, partly hidden in the blueberry bushes was a deep, ominous opening — a dark crater. She'd almost fainted with fear. Rose then had hollered and hollered the children's names into that godforsaken hole, but there was no reply.

Knowing how deep the bootleg pits could go, she'd realized that a further cave-in would trap her children forever. Regardless of the danger, her first impulse had been to slide into the opening and find her family, but then she'd have been trapped, too. She fought off those feelings of panic and then bravely ran to find help.

The closest house to Fox farm was actually at the edge of the open field. After Rose had explained her predicament to the woman who'd answered her poundings on the back door, phone calls were made — to friends, townspeople, her husband's mining buddies. People and equipment began arriving throughout the night with generators and lights that transformed the darkened sky. Bushes were cleared, tents and portable toilets set up, but no active digging could start until dawn; the risk of a cave in was just too high.

"When is your Buddy coming home, Rosie?" asked Sadie, interrupting Rose's thoughts with a welcome distraction.

"He should be here around 8:00 tonight," Rose replied. "The United Mine Workers Union paid for an airline ticket to bring him home on short notice."

"Miners are a close-knit bunch, eh?" Sadie said with pride. Her husband, a former miner, was working a backhoe, carefully widening the opening into the pit. He'd found a job with a construction company when number 26 Colliery closed.

"How did he take it?" Sadie continued. "The news, I mean."

"Well, you know how Buddy is," Rose began. "Silence at first, followed by a few cuss words about how irresponsible kids are. Then he asked how I was doing, said to hang tough and he'd be on the first plane home."

"I imagine he'll find the flight long."

"Oh, yes," agreed Rose, "he's a doer, not a watcher."

The hills quieted in anticipation as the four-man rescue crew readied to enter the pit. Clad in helmets and masks with oxygen tanks strapped to their backs, the men, side-by-side, grasped thick ropes to rappel down into the darkness. Ventilation hoses were already in the cavern, exchanging air and removing dust. Lights would be sent down next.

Rose fidgeted and prayed as the minutes dragged by. "Please, please, please …" she whispered repeatedly, her eyes glued to the pit entrance. The wait felt like hours, each minute adding immeasurably to her anxiety.

Mercifully, thirty minutes later, a white-helmeted senior rescue official strode purposefully toward her. Rose stood, hands clasped and heart pounding. "Are they…?"

"They're okay, Rose!" he interrupted her, smiling. "The men are checking them now."

"Oh, thank God," cried Rose, hugging him in gratitude. "They're all right, Sadie," she sobbed. "They're all right!"

Clapping and shouts of joy followed Rose's words, rapidly spreading through the crowd.

"Can I see them? When can I see them?"

The three children simultaneously awoke to the noise of clattering machinery, bright spotlights, and shadowy, helmeted figures. Being familiar with the rescue gear of miners, they weren't afraid. They'd seen their dad in similar clothing.

Everything happened quickly. The children were given oxygen and examined for broken bones. Within an hour of their discovery, the three were strapped on rescue boards and hoisted above ground.

Rose greeted them ecstatically with hugs, and kisses, and tears. "Oh, my babies," she sobbed, moving from Bobby, to Tommy, to Karen. "Are you all right? Does anything hurt?"

The cameraman, grinning, captured the happy reunion.

"Rose, the kids will have to be taken to the hospital for a more detailed assessment," cautioned Charlie Jobes, one of the rescuers, and a friend of her husband. "There were high levels of methane and carbon monoxide in that pit. No wonder they were asleep when we found them."

"Okay, Charlie, just give me a few more minutes."

The three stretchers lay side by side, Karen between her brothers. Rose knelt at her daughter's head. "All this for some blueberries and coal … I hope you kids have learned from this," she said softly, her eyes puffy from crying. "I know I have."

The children, still strapped to rescue boards, nodded at their mother.

"Believe in myself," said Tommy.

"Be truthful," answered Bobby.

"Discipline," muttered Karen. "Self-discipline."

"What?" stammered Rose, frowning quizzically. "What are you saying?"

"Time to go, Rose," interrupted Charlie, helping her to her feet. Workers quickly lifted the stretchers and started moving the children to the ambulances. Further discussion would have to wait.

"We'll … we'll talk more when we all get home," Rose said distractedly as Charlie led her to his car. "Oh, your dad will be home tonight," she added turning her head back to the stretchers. "We'll all talk."

"There are many people to thank," intoned Phonse Johnson to his television viewers, as the camera captured a panoramic shot of the rescue scene — miners, firefighters, police and well-wishers. The cameraman zoomed in briefly on an elderly white-haired couple, arm in arm, smiling serenely.

"And so, a happy ending," Phonse continued, as the ambulances pulled away, sirens blaring. "No loss of life or limb, and lessons learned by all." He pointed to the open pit. "Workers will now begin to fill in and seal off this old mine to prevent any possible repeat of this accident."

He looked confidently back into the camera lens. "From Coal Town, Cape Breton, this is Phonse Johnson, CBN News."

Inside the Triangle

One

"Harvey, I don't like this! Shouldn't Cuba be visible by now?"

"Relax, Janet, we're right on course," said Dad, scanning the instrument panel. "This fog is reducing our visibility, but we'll make a visual any minute."

"We should have seen land ten minutes ago," Mom muttered rechecking the map on her lap.

Harvey reached over and squeezed her shoulder. "I'll give Miami ATC another call."

"Hey, Dad," interrupted Aiden, "the sky looks different."

"Yeah," I piped in, "the colour looks strange, kind of angry." To the right of our Cessna the clouds were an intense yellow-red colour with some purple mixed in. Weird.

"Kiara, Aiden be quiet back there while your dad radios the air traffic controller," Mom ordered, her voice high pitched and tight with worry.

"Miami control," said Dad picking up his radio mike. "This is flight 471. Can you read us?"

Static and a broken up voice replied. "Roger flight 471 … I hear you … cannot pick you … radar. What is … ing?"

"Try again Miami, you are breaking up!" replied Dad speaking rather loudly.

"... zzzz."

"Harvey!"

"It's okay, Janet. We'll just try and raise Havana," he said while switching the radiofrequency. "Hava ... ? What the heck?" The cabin lights flickered on and off and the compass swung back and forth.

"Harvey, those clouds are getting awfully close," said Mom with an edge of panic in her voice.

The plane suddenly lurched down and to the right from a forceful gust of wind. Aiden groaned, I gave a little shriek, and Mom grabbed her chair with a death grip, while Dad fought with the controls trying to steady the plane. "Get your helmets on," he ordered through clenched teeth, "and make sure your life vest is secure ... the wind is really picking up."

Mom grabbed the mike. "Havana air traffic, come in. Come in." No answer.

"Keep trying," said Dad as he struggled to straighten the plane after another gust had shaken the craft. He glanced over his shoulder and nodded approvingly at Aiden and me. We both had our helmets on, as did Mom, and we were now also fiercely holding on to the arm rests. Every time Dad let go of the controls with one hand to put on his helmet, the plane bucked, dipped or veered off to one side or another. "Later," he grumbled letting the helmet drop to the floor.

The sky glowered around us. Black clouds gathered in front and rain started beating on the windshield. Our visibility in almost every direction was, maybe, five meters.

"Can you get above this?" I shouted, "Above the storm?"

"No," Dad replied. He pointed to the gas gauge. "We need to find land."

"Oh, Harvey ...."

"Hold on tight everybody," Dad hollered. "I'll try and go below these clouds for a visual." The plane dipped and shuddered, causing my stomach to lurch.

"Havana air traffic, come in. Come in." Mom kept on trying.

"I don't like this," complained Aiden looking kind of green.

From my seat behind the co-pilots chair I had a clear view of the instrument panel. The altimeter reading dropped from 4000 meters to below 1800 meters without any change in the outside view.

"Harvey," shouted Mom, pointing, "There, in front of us, there's an opening in the clouds." It looked almost like a tunnel through the dark storm clouds. Dad fought to steer the aircraft into the apparent clearing, the strain of the effort showing on his face. Dials on the instrument panel spun wildly and the dashboard lights flashed on and off. For a few seconds, the altimeter read zero and air speed 750 kilometres per hour —both impossible. The right wing dipped, and despite Dad's efforts, the plane went into a dive and spin.

We all started screaming and crying — at least Mom, Aiden and me did — Dad was too busy. He manoeuvred the ailerons, elevators and rudder with determination, frantically attempting to stop the spin. He's done this before, I thought over and over, trying to reassure myself. Time seemed to stretch as I watched him struggle with the controls.

Abruptly, the spin slowed and Dad managed to pull up the nose of the plane and regain some altitude. The fog around us just disappeared. It was like leaving a tunnel, one minute we were in the dark and the next in bright sunlight.

"Harvey, I see land!" Mom shouted. ""Out my window, there's an island."

The plane was finally responding to Dad's movements. "We're going to be okay, he shouted. " We're out of the spin!" Sweat was dripping down his face as he leveled out the plane and headed toward the island. It was heavily treed and had an obvious volcanic origin with a large central mountain evident.

"That was great flying," said Aiden, a quiver in his voice.

"Yeah, Major, you earned your stripes today!" I hollered.

"We don't have enough fuel to go much further," Dad said. "I'm going to land on the beach, so everybody make sure they're strapped in tight and holding on."

Mom tried one more time to reach Havana air traffic control with the radio, but got no response. She twirled the dial to pick up any radio transmissions — nothing. Usually this close to land there was some radio activity.

"The sky's kind of different," I said, looking out my window. "It's all pink!"

"Probably just the storm, Kiara," offered Aiden.

We circled the sandy area twice, gradually losing altitude and reducing air speed. Our shadow got progressively larger on the white sand below. "Okay, everybody, hold on tight," Dad instructed as we angled down. "With the soft shore, I'll have to stall it when we touch down."

Seconds later, the wheels touched down smoothly on the sand and we started to taxi. The ground was too soft. Almost immediately after the front wheel hit the sand, it collapsed and the nose of our plane jammed into the beach. Dad, still helmetless, crashed headfirst into the control panel. Mom also hit the dash, but she did have *her* helmet on. Aiden and I were thrown forward into the back of the front seats, but neither of us hit anything hard or sharp. At least I didn't.

The engine stopped and an ominous silence filled the plane.

Two

I was first to move, unbuckling my seat belt, then pushing open the side door. Manoeuvring was difficult because the tail of the Cessna was high in the air and the cabin tilted forward. Aiden was right behind me, practically falling to the hot white sand. Neither of us was hurt, but we sure were scared.

"A … Aiden," I stammered. "Are you okay?"

He muttered something to the affirmative as we took off our helmets and yellow Mae West vests. Then, despite shaking legs, I pulled open the front doors of the plane to check on Mom and Dad.

"Oh my God!" I cried. They looked … dead. "Aiden, get over here," I ordered, my heart beating wildly.

Mom was slumped forward, with blood all over her face. Her nose looked broken, pushed off-centre and all swollen. But she *was* breathing, and she moaned when we pulled her from her seat and laid her on the sand. She's just a bit taller than my 152-centimetre height, but lying there on the hot white sand, she looked so small and vulnerable. Her left arm was crooked just above the wrist and twisted, but the skin looked okay. Carefully, I took off her helmet and wiped her face with a cloth from the plane. Blood from her nose was everywhere, soaking her flight suit and her long sandy hair. She was breathing normally and her pulse was strong.

Dad was another story. He didn't even moan when we moved him. The right side of his face was bleeding and he had a goose egg of swelling above and in front of his ear. He's a big man – 185 centimetres, 95 kilograms — so Aiden and I had a tough job getting him out without dropping him. But we did it, and then dragged him over closer to Mom. She was starting to make some noises by this time and was moving her legs a bit in the sand. Dad just lay there.

I fought the urge to scream and cry and ... run. Aiden kept saying, "What'll we do Kiara? What will we do?"

I wanted to tell him to shut up, but knew that would only make him worse. "See if you can find some water," I suggested." Then I checked Dad's breathing and measured his pulse. Ten slow breaths per minute and a pulse of about 110 beats per minute. That first aid course sure came in handy.

A canteen pushed in front of my face announced my brother's return. "Oh, God, Aiden," I said, dropping the canteen to the sand. "Look at his right leg!" I said pointing. It was bent at an unnatural angle just below the knee."

The seriousness of the situation suddenly hit me. They could really die.

I kind of lost it for a few minutes at that point, asking Mom and Dad to wake up and talk to me, while tears streamed down my face. Aiden then did something that he'd never done before, that I can remember. He put his arms around me and gave me a big hug. He was crying a bit too, but not as loud as me.

It's not that we don't get along, 'cause we do. But, even though we're twins, we hang with different crowds and have different interests. He's a gamer, hand held, computer, no matter. I'm into outdoors and books. Aiden loves meat. Me, I'm vegetarian. That hug … well, it said a lot.

"They'll be okay, Kiara. Don't worry," he said, hoping more than lying.

"Yeah," I nodded, wiping my tears in my sleeve.

Our silence only lasted a few moments. Inland noises (was it chanting?) turned our attention away from the shore to the tree line behind us. People were moving between the trees and they were walking toward the beach … to us! It looked like thirty or forty anyway. Aiden and I smiled at each other and started waving to the approaching people. Help was arriving!

But as the group of people got closer and we could make out the features of our "rescuers", relief quickly faded. They looked like people from a National Geographic magazine. They were all dark-skinned and the biggest wasn't any taller than me! The men looked fierce though. Most had shaved heads and they were wearing only loin clothes and carrying an assortment of weapons — bows, spears, clubs and knives. Many had jewelery around their necks and multiple bracelets on their wrists and ankles. The women had multi-coloured wrap dresses on and lots of jewelery as well, but they didn't seem to have weapons. Some children were behind the group, peeking out from the palm trees. In front of the whole group was an old man with a long gray beard. He wore a strange hat with feathers sticking out in all directions and odd patterns were painted on his chest. The wooden staff and long shield he carried added to his fierceness. I guessed that he was the leader.

"We need help," I said facing them with my palms turned out to show that I carried no weapons.

The old man said something in a language that I couldn't understand.

"Our parents are hurt," said Aiden pointing to Mom and Dad. "Can you help us?" His voice was steady, I was proud of him.

The crowd slowly moved forward, eyeing us suspiciously. After the old man said something, four of the men cautiously came forward pointing their spears. I couldn't believe they were scared of us. I started to cry and once again, my brother put his arm over my shoulder.

Maybe it was the tears, or maybe the advancing men saw how young we were, despite us being as big as them. They turned to the old man, said something and then put down their spears. The old guy stopped briefly in front of us, looked us up and down and then proceeded toward our parents.

"They're hurt," I said. "We crashed."

The old man placed his ear on my dad's chest and then gave him a once-over exam, feeling his limbs, looking in his eyes, and gently running his fingers over the large swelling above his ear. He said a few words to his people, before moving over to my mom. He then did the same slow careful exam of her, said a few more words, then motioned for one of the children to come forward.

A girl, no taller than my chin, came forward. She had dark curly hair cut close to her scalp and wore a purple and orange swirling sari. Colourful bracelets adorned her wrists and ankles. She exchanged a few words with the old man, then walked toward me, smiling shyly. It was then I decided that these people were friendly and going to help.

Aiden let me go and I walked toward the girl. We looked each other over, and then she patted her chest with her right hand and said, "Murisha."

I followed her lead, patting my chest saying, "Kiara."

She smiled and said my name, and I did the same, saying her name while pointing at her.

The old guy made some noises that sounded urgent. He was kneeling by my dad and he looked worried. A woman passed him some leaves from a leather pouch. He crumbled them up, putting some inside my dad's cheek. When Aiden tried to move forward to question him — it might have been poison for all we knew — two of the men gently but firmly blocked him. They were smiling and motioning with their hands for us to relax. The old man then put some of the leaves inside the cheek of my mom as well.

"Maybe it's a pain killer," I said to Aiden. He nodded, but still looked tense. "We have to co-operate, Aiden. We don't have much choice," I added.

The old man straightened up and came over by me and Murisha. He spoke rapidly — I don't know what he said — and placed our hands palm to palm. Murisha nodded her understanding and smiled at me before running off towards the trees. I just stood there.

Some of the men and women came forward and spoke to Aiden and me. Their smiles seemed friendly but the words made no sense to us. We smiled back, not knowing what else to do. Then two men came from the trees each dragging a stretcher made out of tree branches and vines or plants. The old man spoke rapidly to them and watched closely as they gently placed Mom and Dad on these makeshift frames.

Murisha returned as this was going on, carrying a clay cup filled with a clear liquid — probably water — a large bird's feather and a stone knife. She exchanged some words with the old man, who pointed to me and indicated that I should sit on the sand. I did, and Murisha did the same, sitting cross-legged facing me.

She took the knife and pricked her left index finger. Squeezing it with her other hand, she let two drops of her blood fall into the cup. Smiling, she passed me the knife, her expectation clear. I looked up at Aiden who was standing to my left. "We don't have much choice," he said. "They seem friendly enough so far."

I took the knife and did as Murisha had done. It didn't hurt very much. When the drops of my blood fell into the cup, the surrounding people all murmured what seemed like approval. They all smiled and nodded.

Murisha stirred the cup with the long feather, then after looking to the old man for approval, held the cup to her lips and took a drink!

She passed it to me.

This wasn't something I really wanted to do. I tried to give it back. "I can't drink this," I said out loud. Murisha tilted her head to the side like you do when you have a question, then held the cup back out to me and nodded her head.

"You want me to drink this?" I said making eye contact.

She nodded.

Did she understand my speech? Impossible! "What's my name?" I asked to see.

"Kiara," she replied.

"How ...?"

She smiled and pointed at the drink. I took a big breath, and looked over to Aiden. "She can understand me!" I said. He nodded, but remained silent. Was it the drink? How could that be? My curiosity was getting stronger than my fear, so I reached out, picked up the cup and drank the remains. The people around us clapped their hands as I put the cup down in the sand.

"We have just shared the blood drink of sisterhood," said Murisha. "The feather of the wise owl mixes our blood and allows us to understand each other."

I stared at her my eyes wide with surprise. "Aiden, did you hear that?" I asked my brother.

"Just mumbo jumbo," he answered.

"The drink allows only us to understand each other," explained Murisha. "I hear your words in my language and you hear mine in yours."

"Can they understand me?" I asked looking at some of the other people there.

"No, the potion is only between the two sisters. You must translate me, and I you to our peoples."

My head was busy digesting all this. "Who is the old man?" I asked looking at the gray bearded one.

"That is our shaman, our medicine man. My father," she replied with obvious pride. The Shaman said something to Murisha that was just gibberish to me.

"He wants to know your story," Murisha indicated. "We can talk as we go to our village."

"Can he help my parents?" I asked looking at the two stretchers.

"He will try. He is a powerful shaman; he has great skills!"

"What about our plane?" I asked gesturing behind me.

"No one will touch it. It is foreign."

Foreign, poison, contaminated … multiple words popped into my head when Murisha answered. Weird, but I now knew that our stuff was safe.

We stood. While Murisha talked to her father, I updated Aiden. He, like me was worried and had lots of questions, but at least we could now communicate with these people! Murisha walked on my left and Aiden on my right as we began to move toward and then through the thick trees at the shore. The Shaman was immediately behind us.

"Murisha, what did your father give my parents?"

"It was an extract from a medicine plant that relieves pain and helps make one rest," she answered. "It is very safe," she added to reassure me.

Her father said something. "Tell us what happened," Murisha translated.

So I did. I tried to tell them things I thought they'd understand. You know, things like us four being a family from far away. I told them that our plane was just like their stretchers, something that our people could build. I had to explain that our white skin didn't mean that we were sick and that we all ate plants and sometimes animals as our foods. I told them that we got lost in the clouds and seemed to come through a great tunnel in the sky. The Shaman nodded his head thoughtfully when I said that.

"We have seen flying machines before!" said Murisha after her father had finished quizzing me. "Three times in the last ten cycles — years, I mean. This is the first time that any people survived though."

"Were their planes like ours?" I asked.

"One, I think. The other two were bigger," she replied. "I can show you their remains sometime, if you wish."

I mumbled an answer to show that I'd heard but truthfully, my mind was elsewhere. These villagers have only seen three other planes in ten years? Where the heck were we? This sure wasn't Cuba!

I kept walking.

In a clearing, not far in front of us, was the village. Straw huts surrounded a central fire pit. There were at least forty small homes and three larger buildings. A few children played near the centre and several roosters or chickens strutted around as well.

"Those are meeting rooms and for storage," said Murisha anticipating my questions. "The birds are raised by the villagers and cared for by the children." I nodded. "And over there," she continued, pointing with her left hand, "behind that grove of palm trees, is where we keep our boats and fishing gear."

I translated for Aiden.

"Ask her if I can have one of those drinks," he said.

I asked. Murisha shook her head. "The Shaman does not have a son near your brother's age and only one of royal blood has the gift to perform the blood mixing."

I translated to Aiden. His scowl was understandable in any language.

"He will have to learn our language the hard way," Murisha added smiling.

The Shaman directed the two stretchers be placed inside one of the large huts. He voiced other instructions and in response, two men gathered wood for a fire while some young women went into the forest behind the village — to collect herbs and medicines — Murisha explained.

"What is your father's name?" I asked as I followed my new "sister" into the large hut.

"His name is Sitkeem but nobody calls him that except my mother," answered Murisha. "All of the villager's address him as 'Shaman'."

I turned toward Mom, who groaned, moved her head and opened her eyes. She looked horrible with all that blood on her face and flight suit. I motioned to Aiden and we knelt on each side of her stretcher. "You're gonna be okay, Mom," I said. "We found some help."

She was groggy but her eyes focused in recognition. "Kiara … Aidan …Where's your father? Where's Harvey?" The words were sluggish and slurred.

"Dad's here with us," I started, but Mom wasn't listening. Her attention was on the people behind me. "Who…?" Her eyes widened and she tried to sit up.

"No, Mom," said Aiden, placing a hand on her shoulder. "Don't move. You're hurt." She moaned from the sudden movement and slumped back to the ground. Aiden patted her shoulder lightly. "We're in a village with people who found us at the beach."

"They're friendly," I reassured. "And they're trying to help us."

"Your father?"

"Dad's pretty bad," Aiden said, his voice shaking slightly. "He didn't have his helmet on."

"How bad?" Mom whispered.

I turned to Murisha, who quizzed her father, and then translated for me.

"Mom, you broke your nose and your left wrist," I said. "And Dad broke his lower right leg and probably has a fractured skull."

Mom looked at me suspiciously. "What …?"

"That's what the Shaman says," I added. "He checked you both out before we moved you here."

"Shaman?"

As if on cue, I was motioned aside and the Shaman knelt beside Mom. "Don't be afraid, Mom," I said, seeing again the oddness of the native appearance. "These people are trying to help."

My mother nodded her head. "Okay."

The village leader gently grasped her shoulder and murmured a few words. Murisha and I translated. "Your arm and nose both need to be straightened," he said.

Mom looked at her left wrist, then felt her nose with her right hand and nodded. "We have some medicine to remove the pain and then a splint will be needed." Again my mom nodded.

"Your man needs his leg fixed." The Shaman paused, looking from Mom to Dad and back again. "That is easy. I fear that his head is more serious." He moved to his left giving Mom a clear view of the adjacent stretcher. Mom lifted her head, leaned on her right arm and looked at her resting husband. The swelling in front of and above his right ear was notably bruised and a black eye on the same side was also easy to see.

"Oh, Harvey," she moaned.

"Mom …?"

"Kiara, tell him to go ahead," she whispered lying back on the stretcher. "Set the broken bones, I mean. When I'm better able to move, I can help take care of your father."

After more pain medicine, Mom fell asleep. Aiden and I were gently but firmly escorted outside. "Come back when we finished," instructed Murisha closing the hut's flap. "I help my father."

Aiden and I huddled together by the village fire, shell shocked by the accident, the people, Mom and Dad's injuries … everything. While neither of us wanted to be there when the broken bones were being fixed, we still didn't want to move too far from where our parents were being attended. Everything was so foreign; whispers and staring eyes followed our every movement.

"I know what happened," I said after a long few minutes of silence.

"What?"

"The Bermuda Triangle."

"Go on," Aiden scoffed. "That's just a myth."

"A myth!" I retorted. "Ha! Our flight path took us right into it … and what about the sky?" I asked looking up. "It's pink!"

"That could be from the storm."

"Right." I rolled my eyes. "Look, there's no village like this anywhere near Cuba, is there? You did all the travel agency research."

No, but … I believe Dad," Aiden answered. "He says there's nothing special about the area. It's just an imaginary triangle. Don't you remember what he said?"

"Of course I remember. It was only two days ago that we left home ...."

Three

"Kiara. Aiden. Get your suitcases and put them in the back of the plane."

"Yes, Major," we both answered. Dad didn't like us calling him that, but we did it anyway whenever he was being bossy.

He grimaced at our response, but stayed quiet and even smiled a bit, as me and Aiden put our stuff in the luggage compartment of the Cessna. I guess that nothing, especially a little teasing, was going to interfere with his mood today. He was on vacation, retirement … sort of.

After 20 years in the Canadian Air Force, he'd officially packed it in just two weeks ago. Not that he was really going to retire. Oh no, not my dad. He just loved flying and being busy too much to ever really stop working. He already had a civilian job as a commercial pilot lined up, but was taking a three month vacation before starting in the new plane.

"Honey, can you help me with this?"

That's my mom, Janet. She's thirty-nine, almost five years younger than Dad. Her thick, sandy hair is nearly to her shoulders with a natural waviness that I wished my hair had. The two of them planned and talked about this trip, with each other and us for years. So when they bought the Cessna Skyhawk from one of Dad's pilot friends a few months ago, planning went into high gear. Routes, maps, flight plans, flight gear, a leave of absence for Mom from her nursing position, permission for Aiden and I to leave school three weeks early, and first aid courses for everyone.

"Harvey."

Oh, oh. Dad must be daydreaming 'cause he not answering and he's got that far away look on his face.

"Harvey!" Mom repeated with a touch of impatience.

"Sorry," Dad muttered, still smiling. He shook his head and then went to move a large trunk from the back of the family van into the plane. "I was just thinking about how great all this is."

My father is above average in height – 185 centimetres — and really fit. He runs and does weights and fitness stuff down at the base athletic centre. His crew-cut hair is dark brown, with a little gray at the temples. Aiden, my twin, looks a lot like him having the same blue eyes, hair colour and thin frame but he's not even as tall as me. Twelve years old and I'm already as tall as my mom. I have long auburn hair like hers, but mine is straight and we have the same greenish blue eyes.

"So, Dad," I said poking his arm, "did you finalize our flight plan with the flight office?" Me and Aiden understood and talked the flight language of aircrews. We'd been around airfields and planes since we were babies.

"Yes ma'am, all systems are a go!" he replied, always happy to talk aviation.

"And did you check the weather?" asked Aiden. He was interested in meteorology and liked hearing the flight weather forecast.

"Clear skies all the way, with a slight head wind from here to Philadelphia. We'll check the weather again when we refuel there. Okay, sport?" replied Dad as he closed the luggage compartment.

Aiden and me already knew most of the flight plan by heart. We would make the trip in three refuelling stages; Greenwood to Philadelphia, Philadelphia to Atlanta, then Atlanta to Havana, Cuba.

"Sure Dad, but can I come into the flight offices in the airports with you? I'd like to see the inner operations —if you know what I mean." Aiden responded.

"He wants to be sure that you give the right report," I interjected. About six weeks ago, just after Dad bought the Cessna, he took me and Aiden with him for a brief flight. The winds were higher than he'd reported and the landing was a rough. Since then, Aiden tries to be fully prepared ahead of time. He's like that, cautious and a worrier. Twins we might be, yet we are very different people.

"I've told you both many times," sighed Dad, "the weather report that day didn't mention strong winds!"

"Sure Dad, I believe you," Aiden smiled. "I just want to see how those guys do their jobs."

About thirty minutes later, we were off, airborne, aiming at the clouds. Dad was at the controls, Mom in the co-pilots seat, with Aiden and me in the rear, him on the right. Aiden was playing an electronic game, and I was reading; I always have a book on the go. We all wore tan flight suits and white helmets and when over water, yellow life jackets called Mae Wests. The Major insisted on safety. Why we'd even had family training in first aid and fire safety for this trip.

"That was a smooth take-off, Harvey," said Mom, her voice loud to overcome the engine noises. This was only her fourth trip in the Skyhawk and she still found take offs and landings nerve wracking.

"It's a good plane," Dad replied looking up from the instrument panel. "The guy I bought it from really didn't put too many flight hours on it and he took good care of it." He turned to look at me and Aiden, "Okay people, you can take off the helmets if you want."

"Just put them back on before we land!" added Mom turning toward us. Then to Dad, "When do we go over water?"

Aiden and I both knew all about Dad's air force career and all the planes that he'd flown. He was always telling us flight stories, and taking us to see the flight office and airplane hangars that made up his world, whatever base we were at.

Air turbulence shook the plane, interrupting my thoughts.

"Harvey ...."

"Just a little wind, Janet," Dad said in a matter of fact tone. "Nothing to worry about."

Mom looked pale and kind of green.

Dad made some adjustment to the instrument panel, while still talking to Mom, telling her things that she already knew, just to keep her from being too nervous. "Remember Cold Lake, Alberta, Janet? That's where we met ...."

"And got married ...."

"And had us," I shouted, trying to distract Mom.

"That was where I flew Tutor Jets," Dad said pulling the conversation back to flying. "Now *that* was a fun plane to fly!"

"Fourteen years ago," Mom replied, the strain in her face softening briefly. "I remember those days." She smiled, "You were a pretty cocky guy back then."

Dad laughed, "That type of precision flying sure makes you a better pilot."

"Maybe so," Mom answered," but those two years with the Snowbirds gave me a few gray hairs."

"The Snowbirds are so cool," Aiden piped in looking up from his game.

Blueberries and Coal & Inside the Triangle 117

"You two were only five when we moved to Greenwood, Aiden," Mom said turning. "Do you remember any of the air shows?"

"Not really," he replied, "but I have lots of pictures from back then in my scrapbook!"

Living on an airbase, we got to see lots of air shows. But the only planes we could really remember seeing Dad fly were the Skyhawk, of course, and the Aurora, back in Greenwood. That was a big machine; big and noisy.

"Harvey, I think I like your last plane best," Mom stated.

"That old clunker," answered Dad, his eyes scanning the panel.

"You're reading my mind, Mom," I hollered from the back-seat. "I was just thinking about the Aurora."

"That's a monster plane," Aiden commented, leaning forward.

"Yes," Dad replied, "it's similar in size and controls to the big commercial planes which makes the switch to civilian flying easier."

The plane shifted again in the wind.

"Tell us again about the Aurora?" I asked, trying to keep Mom's mind off the turbulence.

"Well, Kiara, the Auroras provide surveillance along the east coast of Canada, doing patrols to spot illegal fishing, drug runners, and illegal immigrants," Dad replied, briefly looking back at me. "We also watched for submarines or other unauthorized naval vessels in Canadian waters anywhere from the Arctic to off Newfoundland and Nova Scotia."

"You helped out with some search and rescue work, too!" Aiden chimed in.

"Yeah, and medical flights, also," added Mom, warming to the conversation.

Dad moved the controls and steadied the plane after a side wind caused brief buffeting. Then smiling, he answered:

"You're both right. There were quite a few different missions that I took part in the last eight years."

"Yeah, I like the story about the Russian sub you tracked off Newfoundland," Aiden said enthusiastically.

"Remember those Spanish trawlers illegally fishing cod? Mom added.

"That one got in the papers," Dad replied.

"And what about the time you had to land on ice to rescue some stranded sealers up north," Aiden interjected. "That was in the papers too!"

"That one made your scrap book, didn't it Aiden?" Mom said looking back at him.

"Yeah, I think it was in 2003 … ."

"Were you ever involved in a medical rescue, Mom?" I interjected, not wanting this to turn into a 'how thoughtful Aiden was' conversation.

"No hon," Mom responded, shifting her gaze to me. "All my nursing has been ground based. I've no flight experience at all!"

"Your mom helps put 'em back together after I get them to her hospital," said Dad.

Mom laughed, "I've worked in four different hospitals in three different provinces since I met your dad."

"Were you always an operating room nurse?" I queried, leaning forward to hear better.

"Yes, except for a brief time in Cold Lake, where I worked in the emergency room. The changes are good though," Mom continued. "A new job in a different hospital was a challenge that kept me from being bored."

"Maybe after this vacation, you could retire, Mom," said Aiden. "Dad will have a pension and his pay from the new job."

"We'll see," was the answer. It was something that she and Dad had been discussing. I overheard them about a month ago talking about Mom staying home once Dad started his new job. There's not much that happens in our house that I don't know about.

The flight from Greenwood to Philadelphia was just over 1000 km and took five hours. After refuelling, we continued on the second leg of the planned journey to Atlanta, Georgia, about the same 1000 km distance. We were mostly quiet during the flight, as conversation in the noisy cabin took a lot of effort. It was still fun though. From the 3500-metre cruising altitude, we got a great view of the geography below. I liked looking out the window at the small houses and the patterns that the roads and farms made.

By the time we landed, refueled, parked the plane for the night, registered with a hotel, and had supper in Atlanta everyone was tired but excited. We were going to be in Cuba tomorrow! After all that planning, it was finally happening.

Catching a second wind, Aiden and I tried out both of the queen sized beds in our hotel room, bouncing up and down a few times, before receiving the cease and desist order. Even that was done good-naturedly — Mom and Dad were all mellowed out by this vacation.

"… and get ready for bed," Mom directed, still smiling.

"How much farther do we have to go Dad?" asked Aiden while lying on the bed in his pyjamas.

"Just under 1200 kilometres, sport," Dad replied.

"Let's see, we average about 200 kilometres per hour, so … that's another six hour flight, right?" said Aiden his face scrunched in thought.

"We'll be there by mid-afternoon then," said Mom who had just exited the washroom. "It's going to be so nice to walk barefoot along those sandy Cuban beaches."

"I want to go snorkelling," I said trying to hide a yawn. I was already under the covers, but didn't want to miss out on the conversation.

"Are we going to fly through the Bermuda triangle?" asked Aiden.

That got my attention and I sat up. "We are!" I exclaimed. "I've read about that place. Lots of planes and ships disappear there!"

"Now, Kiara," said Mom, "a lot of what you read is just sensationalism."

"Why is it so famous then?" I asked. "One book I read said that more than 100 planes and ships have disappeared in the Bermuda Triangle since 1945, and more than a thousand people are missing or presumed dead!"

Dad laughed. "It's just an imaginary triangle off the southeast Atlantic coast of the United States. Florida, Bermuda and Puerto Rico form the corners and it sits just above Cuba," he said. "And Mom's right, the experts haven't uncovered anything special about the area. Accidents and missing planes or boats happen in many locations with the same frequency as the events in this so called Bermuda Triangle."

"Yeah, but some people think that it *is* mysterious, and that it opens to other worlds or other dimensions," I said, unwilling to give up so easily.

"Alright, everybody," said Mom raising her voice slightly, "it's time for sleep. We have a long day tomorrow, and I don't want our pilot to be tired because he stayed up too late talking about an imaginary triangle!"

"Well, I don't think ...."

"Kiara!" said Mom giving me a warning look.

"Okay, goodnight!" I huffed as I fell back on my pillow.

Four

My remembering was interrupted by Murisha, as she burst from the hut, pushing the beaded doorway aside. "Kiara, where are you?" she shouted, looking all around.

"Here," I responded turning from Aiden.

She easily tracked my voice to the fire pit and moved smoothly toward me. For such a small person Murisha sure commanded a large presence. Her voice, gestures and expressions were mesmerizing, at least to me. Maybe it was the 'blood — sister' thing; Aiden didn't look enraptured.

"Your parents are sleeping," she started, a broad smile lighting her features. "My father has done fine work."

I sighed aloud my relief and started toward the hut. Aiden did likewise.

"No," Murisha said holding up both palms to stop us. "They are resting. Now you come with me," she directed offering her hands to my brother and me. "It is my privilege to show you my home and my people." And just like that our day was changed from worry and waiting to fun as we followed her on an afternoon tour of the village.

"Hillar, Moshin … Kiara, Aiden."

"Goran, Tamiz …."

She took great joy in introducing us to anyone and everyone, pointing and then proudly saying either my name or Aiden's. It made no difference that our words were gibberish to the others, all smiled and welcomed us. A group of little kids joined us showering Murisha with questions that she would ask me, or have me ask Aiden. It was kind of amazing, for how different they seemed from us, how similar we actually were! They were short and dark skinned while we were tall and white. Their clothes were self-made, ours store bought. Our languages were poles apart. Yet they laughed, and smiled, and shared with us, showing the same gestures and emotions as kids from home.

We went to Murisha's family hut and met her mother, Sithlar. She, like her daughter, was quite small, the tip of her head barely reaching my chin. Her gray speckled hair, similar to most women in the village, was cropped close to her scalp. She wore a very colourful and elaborate dress that befitted and designated her status as the Shaman's wife — that's what Murisha said anyway. Vibrant jewelery decorated her neck, forearms, wrists, and ankles. She smiled easily, and offered us some food — fruits and a type of bread — that we hungrily accepted.

By late afternoon I was wearing a green, red, and yellow, wrap dress that Murisha had borrowed from someone and Aiden was prancing about in the loincloth that the boys wore. My long sandy hair was tied up in a multitude of tight braids, while Aidan's light crew cut was died jet black. He and I both had thick woven bracelets on our wrists and ankles. Some flowers scattered in my hair and a tooth necklace of some sort hanging around Aiden's neck completed our 'transformation'.

I don't think that I ever laughed so hard and as often as I did that afternoon. The village children and elders were so friendly and kind.

Blueberries and Coal & Inside the Triangle

By the time we returned to the 'hospital', it was getting dark. The woven stick framework and overlapping thatch roof, water tight Murisha told us, allowed sufficient light inside for us to easily see where we were heading. These people rarely needed candles as their lives cycled with the sun, and, of course, the climate was always mild. The only necessary fire was the central pit and that used for cooking.

Unthinking, Aiden and I rushed into the hut talking excitedly. The Shaman scowled and shushed us to silence as we entered, banishing our laughter. "Quiet, quiet!" he admonished with Murisha translating. "Your elders need rest."

Shamefaced, we looked for my parents. Mom was sitting up, leaning against a pile of animal hides. Surprise registered when she saw us in our native garb, and she gave us a tired smile and winked.

"Are you two really my children?" she asked as we sat beside her. Her voice was really nasal and muffled, like when you have a stuffy nose.

"Everyone has been so nice," I told her.

Somebody must have helped her get washed, because her face and hair were clean, all traces of blood gone. And her nose, though swollen, was once again straight.

"Here, too," she replied. Gesturing to her right she pointed to our father's sleeping form. "Your dad woke a short while ago." She sniffed loudly.

"Is he okay?" asked Aiden, wincing at Dad's swollen features.

Mom nodded, her eyes only half-open. "He asked about you both, but then fell back asleep a short time ago. That plant medicine the Shaman uses is pretty potent," she added.

I looked at her left wrist; it was in a splint made from thick tree bark. Dad had similar material around the leg that he had broken. "How do you feel?" I asked.

"Sore and tired," she admitted, "but thankful to these people for their help. It doesn't seem real, yet,'" She shook her head and then focused her gaze on me. "Kiara, was I imagining it or were you really talking to that girl over there before?" Mom asked, gesturing to Murisha.

Aiden answered. "Mom, that's the Shaman's daughter, Murisha. She and Kiara drank a blood potion that lets them understand each other's speech!"

"What ...?"

I gave a tight-lipped grin and nodded. "Things are different here," I murmured. "You'll see."

"Oh, my!" Mom's eyelids were drooping, and her speech was slurring. "I ... I don't ... understand," she said slowly. "We'll have to talk more ... in the morning, okay?" Her eyes closed.

Rapid gibberish announced the approach of Murisha's father. He was waving some stick with fur, back and forth, while he hummed and muttered. Murisha gestured for us to leave. "Your parents need rest and will stay here tonight."

"I'm staying ...."

"No, my father will guard their spirits and tend their needs," she reassured. "His magic is strong!"

I caught Aiden's eye and translated. He nodded.

"Okay, where do we go?" I asked stifling a yawn. It had been a long day.

"If it pleases you," Murisha responded, "you will stay in the home of my family."

Of course it pleased us. This was just another of the enigmas of our stay in Kikila. Murisha and her family were offering *us* the help but acted as if *we* were honouring them! The formality and courtesies that these 'savages' showed far eclipsed those that I practiced or saw in our 'civilized' world. Regardless, it was very considerate and very much appreciated.

However, I can't say that I appreciated it when Murisha shook me from my sleep the next morning and dragged me outside

Blueberries and Coal & Inside the Triangle **125**

the hut, before the sun was even up! I hardly even knew where I was.

"Hey, stop it. What are you doing?"

"My sister, you must greet the sun with me," she said, showing no sympathy.

"I don't like ...."

"It is necessary," she insisted.

"What about Aiden?" I asked trying to lie down on the sand.

"He is not blood bonded." She tugged on my arm.

"Are you sure that you need me?" I persisted.

"We will honour the day by watching the return of light," she continued ignoring my protests. "We must try and ensure that the gods look favourably on your visit and speed the recovery of your parents."

I couldn't really argue with that, and truthfully, the thin crest of lightness along the bottom of the sky *was* beautiful. Besides, I don't think I'd ever seen a sunrise before, and she had me kind of curious.

My feet followed hers, past the deserted fire pit into the trees behind one of the gathering huts. Everything was very quiet. Murisha and I were up and out before most of the village even started to awaken. "Even the birds are still asleep," I said, one last protest at being awoken so early. Murisha snorted a laugh but didn't turn or slow down. She kept tugging me along until we reached a hill overlooking the ocean and the eastern sky.

"The gods of our land show themselves at this time," she said softly, sitting amidst the lush grasses. "Before the jungle awakens you can truly feel their greatness. Relax, Kiara, my sister. Breathe deeply and feel the power and beauty of the gods."

Now, I don't know what to think of the gods she was talking about, but she *was* right about how beautiful and peaceful the 'return of light' was. I've never seen such a wondrous sight. As the sun crested the horizon and its reflection reached our island birds began their daily music and life awoke. Even Murisha's humming and chanting, odd anywhere else, seemed natural, almost a part of the place.

I was still tired though, and the sky was still pink.

The Shaman met us at the entrance to the hut where my parents slept. He looked kind of drained, but his speech to Murisha was rapid and pointed, accompanied by extravagant gestures.

"What's he saying?" I asked anxiously when he disappeared back inside the hut.

"My father is much worried about your dad," Murisha replied. "He believes that illness is spreading inside your father's head," she continued, "and he feels that something needs be done about it."

"Like what?"

"He needs to let the illness out; he needs to make a hole in the skull where the damage is."

"What?" I blurted.

This didn't sound good. While I was beginning to trust Murisha and her people, the procedure that she described sounded pretty serious and dangerous to me. Especially here, I mean, not in a real hospital.

"Look," I said, "my mom's a nurse. She'll know what to do. Tell your father to hold it for now and I'll talk to my mom."

I pushed aside the beaded door and we entered the hut. The place reeked of incense. Mom was sitting up next to Dad, who was lying on a straw mattress sleeping. She was softly stroking his forehead and whispering to him. Gods ... I wanted to cry.

Mom looked at me as I approached.

"Is Dad okay?" I asked nervously, swallowing my tears.

Mom shook her head. "He's showing signs of having bled into his brain," she answered in a wavering voice. Tears rimmed her eyes.

I moved closer and we hugged each other.

"The Shaman says that Dad needs to have a hole put in his skull to get better," I said.

Mom pulled her head back in surprise. "A burr hole," she murmured lightly touching Dad's temple. "He's right," she sighed reluctantly. "Your father awoke briefly this morning and we talked. The right side of his face didn't move very well, and his left arm and leg are weak."

I waited for her to explain further.

"He's got blood in there causing pressure on his brain and the weakness — and a drill hole would relieve it! How did the Shaman know?"

"He's the medicine man here as well as their leader," I said.

"Let me talk to him, Kiara," Mom said. "Get him, get him now."

I hollered to Murisha and she brought her dad over. He was shaking that stick thing again and muttering, but his eyes were clear and his face concerned. Murisha nodded her head at what her father said and then spoke to me.

"The Shaman says that it's bad spirits causing the problem," I translated from Murisha. "They are trapped inside his skull and ... eating a part of his brain."

"It doesn't matter what he thinks is the cause," Mom replied, "as long as he can do the procedure!"

"He can do it, Mom," I assured her. "He's done more than ten of these drill holes, on people with head injuries, or people seeking some sort of mystical awareness."

"I think I read something about ancient religions doing this," Mom stated.

"He's even done it to himself!" I translated, incredulously. Sitkeem was rubbing the area behind his right ear. "He says that all shamans have the procedure done, as it increases their powers."

This was starting to sound really weird to me, but Mom just nodded, so I figured that it must make some sense to her.

The Shaman shook his stick thing over Dad and hummed rhythmically.

"He's gathering his magic to help your father," whispered Murisha.

Mom checked Dad's pulse and looked at his pupils. Then she rubbed Dad's cheek and kissed his forehead. "Tell the Shaman that he can go ahead but I want to prepare the scalp and care for your father after it is done," she said, fighting to keep her voice steady. "He'll die without the hole being drilled."

The Shaman barked some orders on hearing Mom's decision, then quickly left the hut with Murisha following. "He's going to get dressed for the ceremony," she said from the doorway. "It will take all his skill to save your father," she added with a grim look. "I also, must put on my ceremonial frock."

I hate sickness and I hated seeing my dad so weak. I sobbed in Mom's arms.

"I need you to be strong for me, Kiara," Mom whispered. "There are supplies in the plane that I must have — the first aid kit and your father's shaving gear. Can you get them?"

"Mmhm," I managed, not trusting my voice. Mom squeezed my hand, as I sniffled and got to my feet. After a big breath, I started toward the door. "I'll be quick," I promised.

Rushing through the hanging beads, I almost knocked Aiden over.

"Where are you ...?" he started to say.

"Talk to Mom," I interrupted, not stopping. "I'll be back soon."

Blueberries and Coal & Inside the Triangle

The first aid kit was in the cockpit, while Dad's shaving gear was in the luggage compartment. Both were easy to find and I was back in less than 10 minutes, running both ways. In that brief time, villagers dressed in ceremonial garb began surrounding the hut. They were chanting and slowly walking around the structure as I approached.

"It's to ward off evil," said Murisha who was looking out the door of the hut. "They will perform until my father leaves, after the procedure is complete."

I really didn't know what to think, but I welcomed any and all help.

Within minutes of my return, Mom had Dad's scalp shaved and the bruised area painted with antiseptic. Aiden and I just watched. Outside the chanting grew louder with occasional shrieks and yells. It was kind of creepy.

Absolute quiet announced the Shaman's arrival. He entered the hut wearing a leopard skin shawl around his shoulders and a multi-feathered headpiece. In his hand he reverently held a dark chisel-like tool made from ebony glass. He chanted softly as he approached my father and made some clicking noises.

Murisha, wearing a white sari and an extravagant headdress of feathers, passed him a pouch with his other tools. Her eyes did not stray from her father and her soft humming filled the hut. It was clear that she was his assistant.

Sithlar entered next, moving gracefully next to my mother, wordlessly taking her hand. Mom managed a weak smile of thanks.

Murisha held a bowl of steaming water that the Shaman dipped his black 'chisel' and sharp cutting stones in, before he used them. Mom nodded her head appreciatively at this. "He's sterilizing them," she said aloud, "less risk of infection."

The pressure relieving procedure itself, only took about fifteen minutes. I didn't want to watch, but I had to stay in the hut to translate as Mom and the Shaman tried to communicate. Aiden waited outside during the actual 'operation', joining the villagers who were chanting and circling the hut. I think it made him feel useful.

The grating noises of the "drill" on my dad's skull almost made me sick. When it finally ended the Shaman gave an ear-piercing shriek and clapped his hands about fifteen times. Bloody fluids immediately drained through the burr hole, slowing to a trickle after only a minute or two. The Shaman then took some sort of bony needle and thread (? hair) from the now cool dish his daughter still held. While humming and chanting he sewed the scalp incision back together.

My mom quietly shook her head at the rituals, but otherwise seemed pleased with the skills demonstrated. When the Shaman bowed his head and stepped aside, she quickly moved closer to Dad. After inspecting the burr hole site and the stitching, she cleaned him off, poured more antiseptics on his scalp, and wrapped him up in white gauze bandages.

"It went very well, Kiara," she said after she'd finished. "The Shaman really *did* know how to do a trephination — that's the word for drilling the burr hole. There was a blood clot, like I thought, causing pressure on your father's brain. The hole let out the blood and now I think your dad will be getting better ... I hope so anyway," she added in a shaky whisper.

Both Aiden and I hugged her.

Even with the purplish-green bruising around his right eye, Dad looked better with the clean bandage. I think his breathing was more regular and normal as well. But then, sometimes you see what you want and I really want him to get better.

Five

"Did I not tell you, my sister?"

I grunted assent from my seat in the sand near the damaged Cessna, and nibbled on the pineapple Murisha had provided. Fruits grew everywhere in the surrounding jungle. It was like having a fresh fruit market in your backyard!

"The gods listened and they guided my father's hand! He is a great magician."

"It wasn't magic," I finally retorted, wiping pineapple juice from my mouth with the back of my hand. "The hole let out a blood clot, not evil spirits."

"Perhaps," smiled Murisha unmoved by my unbelieving.

Regardless, the trephination *did* work, relieving the pressure on Dad's brain. Just a few hours after the procedure, he awoke for a brief spell and was able to speak in a pretty clear voice. He also showed better movement of his left arm and leg.

"That black stone my father used comes from the volcano," Murisha said. "It is very strong and very sharp!"

"It would have to be," I murmured, "to cut through bone."

Mom was very impressed by the surgical skill demonstrated by the Shaman. After Dad's brief wakeful spell post burr hole, she actually cried with relief when he fell back asleep. "He's going to be okay."

Sithlar patted her shoulder while humming some sort of tune and Sitkeem waved various hand held totems over Dad's head — to ensure healing Murisha informed us. Aiden and I tried to comfort Mom but were unceremoniously shooed outside the hut by Sithlar. "She need rest; you two need play. Go." Murisha translated dutifully. "I will attend your mother."

"Mom ...," I said looking back from the door.

Mom nodded. "Just check in every now and again," she, said still sniffling.

"We will, Mom," promised Aiden.

Just knowing that Mom and Dad were safe and being cared for let Aiden and me relax. Kikila became our vacation paradise and all the kids our guides. Even though I tried, Murisha was the only Kikilian that I could talk with. No matter how hard I practiced, her people's language was impossible for me to master. Even simple words only stayed in my head for brief moments. Murisha was having the same trouble with English, while others of her people were already mimicking some common phrases like 'hello' and 'good night'. Aiden picked up the new language like he was born to it, making loads of new friends. Predictably, the newfound closeness that he and I discovered waned. Our interests had always been different despite the twin thing and he found my blood status communication issues frustrating.

It didn't matter. Murisha was the sister I'd always wanted and we quickly became inseparable. The Shaman explained that our blood ceremony spiritually bonded the two of us, preventing the actual learning of each other's language. This sharing of blood could not be undone, even if we wished it

Blueberries and Coal & Inside the Triangle   133

so. There were some potions, not without risk mind you, that might separate the language thing, but the sister awareness was forever.

Those first few days were a blast. Everything was new. We climbed tall trees, swam in the ocean and in nearby rivers, ran through grassy fields, trapped and examined local insects and small animals — we had a ball! Aiden and some of his new friends sometimes accompanied us, but for the most part we redeveloped our long standing separateness. Maybe it was an unconscious desire to be individuals rather than twins, or maybe we were just different. I don't know.

When we explored the beach, I'd gather shells and do sketches while he'd dig for clams. While I learned about herbs and medicinal plants in the jungle with Murisha and her father, he went fishing in the forest stream near the village with some of the boys. Like all the village kids, we both collected fruits and fallen tree branches for fuel and helped tend vegetable gardens. Aiden got interested in spear making and throwing while I learned how to dye my skin (for ceremonies) and make saris. Days were full, and life seemed good. A full week passed. Then, a second.

"Hi, Kiara," said Dad, as I pushed through the beaded doorway, arriving for my daily afternoon visit. The hut was quiet and he was alone, sitting on a low bench. I moved closer and gave him a hug, careful not to bump his splinted leg. Then, noticing two finely crafted tree branches on the ground beside him, I said, "Nice crutches."

Laughing, he picked them up, stood and slipped the crutches expertly into their working position. "Sitkeem had one of his woodworkers make these." He traversed a big circle in the hut like a pro, grinning like a kid. "Pretty good, hey?"

"Awesome," I replied, happy that he was in such good spirits. It had been a rough and painful couple of weeks for him.

He sat back on the bench next to me. "Kiara, your hair is back."

"Yeah," I smiled shaking it about. "The braids were a fun change but I like it better shoulder length and loose."

"Me, too," said Dad smiling. "Now you look more like the you I know."

"Does that hurt?" I pointed at his right temple area. His brown hair was just faintly visible and his bruises still glowed, but after everything, he really looked great sitting next to me smiling and talking.

"Naw," he answered rubbing the area with his fingertips. "It's a little numb actually." He grabbed his crutches and stood, starting toward the door. "Come on outside for some fresh air."

As I followed, his outfit registered. "Where did you get those?" I asked noting khaki shorts and a colourful Hawaiian shirt. "I thought you were only issued pyjamas."

"Well, now that I'm mobile, and I'm not really into loin cloths," he answered, making a funny face, "I had Aiden and his friends rescue my luggage. Call me old fashioned ... but I want good old store bought Canadian goods!"

I laughed as we carefully made our way to the fire pit, and sat under the shade of a large palm tree. It didn't look easy using crutches in sand.

"Where's Mom?' I queried, breaking the brief silence. "It's not like her to stray too far from her favorite convalescent."

"With Sithlar," he answered. "They get on really well. I told her that I was fine and I knew you'd be by. She said she'd have Sitkeem check in on me."

"They are all so nice," I replied.

We talked about small things for a few minutes. Some of the stuff I was doing with Murisha, how well Aiden could speak

Blueberries and Coal & Inside the Triangle   **135**

Kikilian, the food and even the weather. I was determined to stay away from home conversations. While me and Aiden, and even Mom (a little) were quite happy in our new existence, Dad really missed Greenwood.

Shuffling footsteps from behind us announced the Shaman's arrival. "'Allo, 'arvey," he voiced proudly. Dad answered the greeting in Kikilian, mumbo jumbo to me, but Sitkeem responded with a broad smile.

They bantered back and forth, using pantomime more than words to communicate. When pieces of wood and a sharp stone blade ended up in Dad's hands, it was time for me to leave.

"Looks like I'm taking up woodcarving," he said, as I gave him a hug. "Part of my rehabilitation." The Shaman was nodding his head vigorously at Dad's smile and acceptance of the gift.

I gave them both a thumbs up gesture and then went off to find Murisha.

A week later, after a lot of practice, Dad could reliably maneuver through the loose beach sand. Of course the first thing he wanted to do now that he was mobile was check the plane. So, with Aiden and me on either side of him, we did just that. It was level now, no longer nose down in the sand, thanks to some of the villagers. The front wheel support was broken, the propeller snapped on one side, and the fuel tank was almost empty. Other than that, the Cessna looked to be in good shape, but without supplies and tools, there was no way home. Dad couldn't hide his disappointment.

It was then I remembered. "Dad," I said, "Murisha told me about other planes that crashed on the island. Maybe there are some parts and fuel at those sites."

His whole being brightened. "Really? Well that might change things," he murmured, more to himself than me. "Yes,

yes, yes." He rubbed his hands together. "We'll have to check those sites."

All the way back to our hut he quizzed me, question after question. Bored, Aiden took off to find his friends.

"Dad!" I finally pleaded, "I don't know any of those things."

"Right," he said, disappointed.

"But, I'll find Murisha," I said and was rewarded with a great Dad smile.

Turns out, I didn't have to look at all. Murisha was waiting at the hut entrance.

"You have questions, my sister?"

"How did she know?" asked Dad, catching the intent of her speech.

"Magic," I said, smiling impishly. "Our blood bond is working."

We all sat on a bench made of tree branches, in front of the now, Fox family hut. Murisha spoke rapidly and the expressions she used went beyond the simple vocabulary that Dad understood, so, I translated. "There are three crash sites. All are within relatively easy walking distance, and Murisha thinks that one, or maybe two of the planes, look a bit like ours."

Predictably, that got Dad pretty excited. Questions came fast and furious. If he could walk without help or the crutches, I think he would have gone right then to find the downed planes. He started to pace back and forth on his crutches trying to formulate a workable plan.

Mom came out of the hut having overheard most of the conversation. "Don't even think about it, Harvey," she warned reading his mind. "You still have about three weeks before that splint comes off."

Murisha bowed toward my parents. "I will take Kiara to these sites," she offered.

I started to translate, but wasn't needed, her intent was clear.

Blueberries and Coal & Inside the Triangle   **137**

"Will you?" asked Dad sitting back down.

"By yourself?" my mom queried.

"Wow, you guys are getting good," I murmured, a bit jealous of their understanding.

"Of course, I will check with the Shaman and seek his blessing," Murisha said. "But be assured, I am very trusted in these things."

I translated.

Both my parents looked skeptical. "Aren't there wild animals out there?" asked my mom, gesturing toward the jungle.

I repeated this question to Murisha.

"The paths that we must travel are safe," she replied. "They have all been blessed by my father."

My parents both shook their heads. They needed more assurance before they'd let me go any distance into the jungle with just Murisha as a guide. After a few minutes of back and forth chatter, Murisha bowed, smiled, and ran off to get her parents.

"They will convince your Mom and Dad, Kiara," she said before leaving. "Just you wait."

As usual, my little sister was right. Sithlar and Sitkeem did eventually convince my parents that Murisha was correct in all her claims. She *was* trusted to travel along the blessed paths *and* the paths were safe."

I was given permission to go and then a lecture about being careful.

"Come on, Kiara," Murisha cajoled. "We have just one day."

I grunted and tried to match her pace. The sun was just cresting the eastern horizon. "Mornings are not my best time," I replied.

Murisha snorted in disgust, forging on. Her short legs showed no mercy.

We didn't carry any gear. "The island will provide," Sitkeem had assured my parents. Fruits and edible plants grew all along our route and rivers were pristine sources of water.

Ferns and grasses lined the thin dirt trail we followed through the tropical forest. Animal noises and bird chatter accompanied us, adding to the magic of the day. Murisha chattered happily as we walked, not at all concerned with the dense jungle and shadowed areas. She carried a spear — "just in case"- but clearly did not believe it would be needed. She had explored the island in its entirety many times, either with friends, or with her father as he searched for various medicinal herbs.

"It *is* safe Kiara," she reassured me, "as long as you keep your eyes and ears open and don't stray from the main path."

The first crash site wasn't of any use. We found it about 90 minutes from the village, deep in the forest. The plane, larger than ours, had exploded on hitting the ground and what was left of it was beyond any further use.

"No one could have survived that!" I said, standing near the impact crater. Murisha just shook her head and turned away, leading me onward.

While we walked, I taught her a bit about flying and the basic parts of a plane, using our Cessna as a guide and pantomiming a great deal. Anybody watching would have thought I was pretending to be a bird. We laughed a lot, but Murisha caught on quickly. Sometimes she'd pretend not to understand just to watch my antics. By the time we were close to the second site, it was late morning. With her new understanding of airplanes, Murisha figured this one wasn't what we needed, either. "It is similar in size to your Cessna," she said, "but it has only one seat with a glass covering and two propellers, one on each wing." Knowing her, she was probably right, but I still needed to see the plane myself, just to be sure.

Blueberries and Coal & Inside the Triangle   **139**

We had to walk through two small streams and then skirt around a swamp-like area to get to the wreck site. There were trees everywhere except for the spot where the plane had come down. The wreckage was almost hidden in the foliage but enough fuselage was visible to identify it as an old World War I German plane. The wings and sides were all corroded and the front end of the cockpit was caved in, resting against the rising volcano wall.

As we neared the plane, my stomach felt queasy. "What if there are some … remains?" I worried. Murisha laughed at my hesitation explaining that jungle scavengers had taken care of that problem a long time ago.

Relieved, I swallowed my apprehension and climbed all over that plane looking in every nook and cranny for useful items. I found a small toolbox with various wrenches and other tools behind the pilot's seat. Knowing that Dad would find a use for any tool, I tucked them back under the seat to retrieve on another day.

To reach the third and most recently downed plane, we needed to cross to the other side of the volcanic mountain. It crashed almost two cycles ago, during very bad weather. One of Murisha's tribesmen witnessed the event and brought some villagers the next day to examine the site. Murisha and her father were part of that group.

The plane had attempted to land on the shore, but strong winds twisted its wings and it crashed in the shallow water of a small ocean inlet. The villager who witnessed this thought that a great bird had fallen and was very surprised to discover humans inside it. The occupants had either drowned or died from the impact.

"This one might be good," Murisha said as the tale was finished. "Maybe it is even a Cessna, like yours."

Narrow paths brought us to the base of the islands central volcano. It was called Zareton to the natives, which meant life-giver, an accurate name when you think about how a volcanic island grows. The lava from eruptions, build up layer on top of layer, until a landmass is formed in the sea.

Old Zareton had been "sleeping" for many years with rare rumblings and occasional smoke arising from its summit. The Shaman told stories of more vigorous shaking when he was a boy but there hadn't been any eruptions for three or four generations.

As we walked around the volcanic base, the narrow path rose and fell in height. Sometimes we were above the tree line, and the view was spectacular. The ocean stretched off in all directions shimmering in the sunlight and casting a clear turquoise colour. Off in the distance (? north) was a small speck of land that Murisha identified as another island. Other people did live there but contact was very rare, as the seas were treacherous and the distance deceptively far. To her knowledge, the people from that island were friendly.

By early afternoon we were getting close. The path descended to sea level leading us once again to thick forest. Vines hung from the branches above us and fronds of fern-like plants reached across our narrow course. "Stay on the path," cautioned Murisha, "there are a great number of snakes around here." She laughed as I suddenly halted, looking around with eyes wide.

"I *hate* snakes!" I said, with a whole body shiver.

"They aren't poisonous," she replied, which reassured me only a bit.

The forest thinned, allowing me a glimpse of water through the branches. Sounds of the shore replaced the rustling of leaves. Waves were higher and the current stronger on this side of the island, Murisha explained. Quite abruptly, we passed from the forest onto the sand of the coastline.

Directly in front of us was a modest sized bay, circular in shape, formed by sand and scattered volcanic rock of varying sizes. The bay was only open to the ocean by a three or four metre channel, but had an overall size similar to the hockey rinks we have in Canada. Tall trees lined the beach, with thick jungle foliage between the trunks. In the water, maybe three metres from the shore, a yellow tail fin marked the watery grave of a small plane.

"At high tide the fin is completely covered, but at low tide the wings just clear the water surface," Murisha stated as we reached the shore. "There were two people in the plane," she continued, "still in their chairs when we found them. My people buried the bodies over there." She pointed to a small hill of sand further down the beach. I shuddered, thinking how it could have been me and my family.

We snacked on fruit while waiting for the water level to fall, then waded into the warm, turquoise water. Even with half of the fuselage covered, it was easy to see that Murisha was accurate in her observations. The plane *was* a Cessna, probably an earlier version of our Skyhawk. The propeller and front wheels looked and felt solid. In fact, aside from some salt streaking and early corrosion, the plane looked in surprisingly good shape.

"Woo hoo!" I shouted, "It's perfect."

"I am glad for you," Murisha answered.

"We'll have to get this pulled out of the water," I said, with enthusiasm. "I'm sure that my dad can use these parts to fix our plane."

Murisha silently climbed down from the wing and started wading back toward the shore. I could feel her sadness.

"Wait, Murisha," I cried jumping into the water. "Wait."

My eventual leaving really bothered her. It bothered me too, but I knew that my family *had* to get back home. Being here wasn't so bad for Aiden and me, but it was very difficult for Mom and Dad. I squeezed her hand in mine as we reached the shore, letting her know that I understood.

The melancholy mood didn't last too long, only a few seconds in fact. As we neared the path leading away from the shore, a loud cat screech filled the air. "A tiger!" exclaimed Murisha, her entire body now alert. "It must have made a kill." She hoisted her spear.

I don't know if it was the noise or just the thought of such a large cat nearby, but I was pretty nervous. Looking back at Murisha, I started to run along the path that we'd arrived on. "Let's hurry," I yelled, pushing forward into the overgrown path. "Let's get back to the village!"

"Be careful, Kiara!" Murisha shouted. "It is safe; my father has blessed it. There is no danger as long as we stay on the path. And slow down, you might ...."

Too late. In my haste, I tripped over a vine crossing the trail and fell forward and off to the right, tumbling down a small ravine. Luckily, I didn't hit any rocks or trees and I don't think I hurt anything. "I'm okay," I hollered to Murisha as I stood up and dusted myself off. Then I saw it ... a one metre long black and orange striped snake was writhing beside my left foot. I screamed loudly, as its teeth sank into the fleshy part of my left calf.

In a flash, Murisha stood beside me. She grabbed the snake with one hand, just behind its head, and applied pressure with her thumb until it let go of my leg. Angrily, she threw it into the trees. "These snakes don't usually bite!" she said sharply, concern etched on her face. Blood dripped down my leg, while tears dripped down my cheeks.

Murisha dragged me back onto the path. "The snake had a nest, there," she said looking back to where I had fallen. "You were unlucky, Kiara. Most times noise scares these snakes off." As she was saying this, she pulled plants out of the ground and in a smooth motion took a hand full of the exposed moist soil and applied it to my wound. "It will be sore, but there is no poison."

Blueberries and Coal & Inside the Triangle   **143**

I nodded, and slowly regained my composure.

The return trip was otherwise uneventful. My calf swelled a little and my limp slowed us, but we made it back to the village at dusk, a few minutes before heavy rain started to fall.

SIX

"Drink up, big sister," Murisha ordered passing me a foul smelling drink.

I sniffed and must have made a face because Murisha giggled. Dipping my tongue in the red 'medicine' confirmed my impression. It tasted horrible.

"What's in it?"

"Boiled snake tongues and bark from two different trees," Murisha said smiling evilly. "It's a healing tea."

I made another face then gulped the down concoction, shuddering as I finished. "You were kidding about the snake tongues, right?"

She just smiled.

My leg hurt. The skin near the bite marks was red and my entire calf swollen. Last evening the Shaman checked me over, muttering and mumbling as he worked. He agreed with his daughter that there was no poison but he said swelling from the bite could still be pretty bad. He was right!

The crushed plants he'd pasted on my leg deadened the pain letting me sleep but I had to crawl to the bathroom this morning. Murisha, his number one assistant, put a new poultice on when I crawled back, laughing whenever I moaned.

"You're supposed to show sympathy!" I half shouted, trying not to grin. Murisha laughed harder.

The Shaman figured that with 'medicine' I'd be back to normal in four or five days although I'd always have the teeth marks as scars. I guess it could have been worse. Mom watched everything he did, questioning his choices but generally agreeing with his instructions.

Murisha stayed with me during my recovery. We shared stories about each other's worlds, laughing at our differences and sharing our similarities. She tried to imagine our society of machinery, computers, automobiles and large buildings but it was just too foreign. It didn't matter anyway, that was there and we were here. The world of Kikila was what we shared. Murisha showed me how to weave grass mats and grass skirts those first two days. Her nimble fingers made magic, mine … well, I was learning.

By the third day I was more mobile, though still limping. We gathered nuts, roots, and berries from the area close to the village and Murisha showed me how to make different colour dyes used in dress making and in ceremonies. We entertained ourselves and everyone else, by painting our faces with some of the dyes we made, creating fierce and funny results. On the fourth day, Murisha helped me make my own bow and some arrows and we practiced shooting targets for hours at a time. Time passed quickly.

During my days of 'rest', Aiden, with several of his friends and some of the men from the village rescued the submerged Cessna from the lagoon pulling it up onto the shore. The gas tank was still intact, didn't have any noticeable leaks, and was almost half-full. This news, together with the tools from the other crash site made my dad very happy, but also very impatient. He wanted to go on a trek NOW and salvage the repair parts that he needed for *our* Cessna. Like a caged bear, he'd pace back and forth with his crutches, only one thought on his mind ... how to get home.

Mom, now fully healed and splint free had to rein him in.

"Harvey, that splint of yours needs another two weeks before it comes off," she told him. "Then you'll need another week or two of exercise before going off into the jungle!"

"Janet ...."

"Ask Sitkeem if you don't believe me."

Dad snorted, but knew she was right. His balance and strength needed time to recover. Overall he looked a lot better though. The burr hole was now hidden beneath new hair, and his black eye was history. Even so, Dad hated being inactive. Thankfully, Murisha's father spent time with him.

Mom was becoming close with Sithlar, spending parts of each day with her. They constantly discussed each other's society and beliefs and helped each other with 'chores', communicating in English, Kikilian, and charades. They only rarely needed Murisha and me to translate anything.

As soon as he got 'medical' clearance, Dad organized a trip to the lagoon. Six villagers, Aiden, one of his friends — Zarwa, I think — Mom, Murisha and me, all went with him. Using stretchers, we managed to carry back all the parts that Dad disassembled from the wreck. He was like a kid at Christmas, wanting everything, but having to choose only a few things. Finally, he settled on the front wheel support, the propeller, the gas tank and some other minor parts that he took just in case.

In the days that followed, the clanging of his hammer began to blend in with the usual village noises. While he fixed the plane, Aiden and I were put in charge of making a runway. The villagers and our friends helped us clear all the stones, rocks and plants from a long section of the shore just above the high tide water line. Dad felt it was firm enough for the plane to taxi on and take off from.

"We're getting close, Janet," he said during our evening meal. "The gas from the wreck was clean and transferred to our plane earlier in the week and the front wheel is straight with the new supports."

"And the runway is done," added Aiden.

Mom and I kept quiet.

"The propeller needs to be switched and then we just had to wait for favourable weather to make our flight home," Dad continued, excited. "There's enough fuel, too!"

That evening, lying on the beach, Murisha and I watched the sun set. I told her about Dad's progress, wanting to help her … and me, prepare for our separation.

"The plane is almost ready," I sighed. "We'll … we'll be leaving soon." I squeezed her hand. "It's been the best eight weeks ever."

Murisha just stared at me with her big dark eyes, digesting my words. Then finally, "The Mountain won't let you go," she replied.

"What do you mean?" I queried, suspecting a joke.

"My father draws his power from the gods within the Mountain and they have told him that you are not to leave."

I sat up and looked at my friend's face. She was serious.

"Murisha, how can you believe …?" I stopped, not wanting to offend her. "Look, in our world, gods don't seem to care much what people do. Why would your god be different?"

"The Mountain god has been our guide and provider for countless generations," she answered. "My father was able to create the safe paths that you and I traveled using some of His energy. In the same way, my father, like all shamans before him can 'talk' with the god about problems."

I waited for her to continue. Part of me wanted to laugh, but another part recognized that the sky above us was not part of the Earth that I knew. Maybe the 'rules' here *were* different.

"You have been touched by our power; you are a blood sister," she said, her eyes filling with tears. "You cannot leave!"

Murisha was genuinely upset, so I squeezed her shoulder to help sooth her. "Maybe we can talk to this Mountain god and ... explain things," I said softly. "I mean, nobody told me that drinking that — stuff — would mean I'd have to stay here forever!"

My little sister straightened as she considered my words. "Yes," she whispered. "We can try." Her forehead crinkled in a thinking pose. "We will need some fruit from the Seeing Tree," she murmured, "and we'll have to get my father's consent and blessing." She paused, looking at me. "It could be dangerous." Her eyes sparkled with excitement.

I didn't really think that talking to a mountain or volcano was dangerous, but what did I really know about these things. Maybe Murisha was right. Maybe there was a spiritual guide within the volcano … I mean; we *were* inside the Bermuda triangle.

"Okay," I agreed aloud, silently wondering what to tell my parents. Like, how could some Mountain god keep me here?

My answer was what Murisha needed to hear. Smiling widely, she wrapped me in a spontaneous hug. Gods, I was going to miss her.

Blueberries and Coal & Inside the Triangle

Seven

Similar to home, meals in Kikila were usually each family's individual responsibility. Carefully tended gardens provided vegetables akin to our potatoes, carrots, onions and beans. Fruit grew everywhere and in abundance — pineapples, coconuts, oranges, pears — to name only the few I recognized. Men and children obtained meat through fishing or hunting. Small game like pheasant, rabbit or squirrel afforded the bulk, but once every few weeks a wild boar or deer would feed the entire village. When such fortune occurred, everyone would surround the village fire pit and share the slow roasting meat. These events brought great pride to the huts of successful hunters.

"Pretty good, huh?" Dad yawned and stretched.

All four of us lazed in the sand near the Cessna, recovering from the feast.

"I like the dancing and storytelling more than the meat," Mom commented, sitting next to him. She had only tried it to please Sithlar. Mom was vegetarian like me.

"Yeah, but meat cooked over hot coals tastes better than stuff in Greenwood," said Aiden. "Except when you make it Mom," he added hastily.

Mom rubbed his light brown hair, now almost to his shoulders. "You better say that," she laughed.

I sighed. Usually, I might comment that I thought eating meat was disgusting, but today more important things concerned me.

"What's up, hon?" Dad asked seeing my restlessness.

"Well," I started, "do you really think we'll be able to get home? I mean, is that going to be safe?" I pointed to the Cessna.

He put his arm around my shoulder. "It works fine. Once the new propeller is on, it should fly perfectly. "More importantly," he asked, "Are you ready to go?"

I hesitated, aware that Mom and Aiden were also listening. "I'm having a really great time," I replied softly, looking at my feet, "and I'll miss Murisha more than you could ever know." Tears filled my eyes, betraying me.

His arm gave me a squeeze. "Friends always stay with us, in here," he said pointing with his free hand to his heart.

"But I won't even be able to write to her," I answered, starting to sob.

Mom's arms encircled me. "It's okay to cry, my sweets," she whispered. "You love Murisha." I sobbed louder.

"Kiara, we have to go back," said Aiden. "Our lives are in Greenwood. Our home and friends are all there."

"I *know* that," I growled, glaring at him. "But that doesn't take away the pain feel."

"Quiet, Aiden," cautioned Dad.

All conversation ceased for a few minutes. The rippling of waves and calls of the gulls soothed me.

"We *do* have to talk, Kiara," whispered Mom, gently drying my eyes.

Blueberries and Coal & Inside the Triangle   **151**

"I know." Sigh.

Dad cleared his throat. "Sitkeem told me that every five to six months a weather system like the one on the day we got here, happens," he began. "First, the sky becomes more deeply pink with purple streaking, then, a dark horizontal funnel cloud forms in the west, and it slowly moves east." He paused. "To leave, we have to fly into that funnel."

"That sounds dangerous," I said.

"We'll only ever have one chance to get back, Kiara," he continued. "If we try and miss the funnel, there's no more fuel."

"When?" I asked thinking of Murisha and the Mountain god.

"Sitkeem expects such weather later this week."

My whole body shuddered. "That's too soon," I complained.

"We've been here five months and a week," said Aiden. "I love it here, too, but it's time to go home."

"Spend all the time that you want with Murisha over next few days," Mom said, patting my shoulder, "but if you see any signs of a storm, stay in the village."

"But I can't leave her."

"You have to come home with us, Kiara," Aiden said, a catch in his voice. "You belong with us."

I could tell that he meant it. For all our differences, Aiden loved me. Touched by his genuineness, I nodded silently.

Dad cupped my chin in his hand and locked his eyes with mine, "We're *all* going home. All of us."

"Everything will work out," Mom added.

They all knew, I realized. The Shaman must have told them.

"The Mountain god … you know?"

"Yes," Mom nodded. "Go on your trip."

"It can't hurt," added Dad.

"Just be back on time," said Aiden. "And try not to get bitten."

I almost gave an angry retort, but saw his smile first. Gulping, I mouthed my thanks, understanding that my family was giving me space and permission to ... say goodbye. The trip with Murisha would be a private, final, shared experience. Period. I mean, think about it, how could anyone not from here even consider that the mountain god was real?

Native superstition ....

Eight

I awoke early; the hut was dim, not dark. Mom, Dad, and Aiden looked to be sleeping as I rolled off my straw mattress and dressed in my favourite orange and green sari. Quietly, I slipped outside to a beautiful sunrise and clear pink and yellow sky. Stretching, I turned toward Murisha's hut, anxious to get started.

She was already outside, waiting expectantly. "Hello, my sister," she whispered. "You're late."

"Right," I muttered, sticking out my tongue as I gave her a good morning hug.

"What's in there?" I asked noting a wicker backpack on the ground beside her.

"Some rope, cooking stuff, bread and a few other things," she answered. "It's a long walk so I am well prepared." She passed it to me. "This, you will carry," she instructed.

"Okay," I agreed, lifting it to my shoulders. "And the bow and arrows?"

"Ah ... insurance," she laughed lifting the quiver and bow.

"Are there any ... snakes?" I shuddered.

Murisha just laughed.

The trail inland was little used, showing overgrowth of grasses and ferns. Of course Murisha led, setting a fast pace. "Stay close, Kiara," she warned. "This path is not one of the protected."

"Why not?" I demanded, creeped out by the foliage rubbing against my legs.

"It is not used enough to merit that attention," she replied. "But my father has given to me a blessing of safety that will keep us both safe as long as you stay close."

"Well, maybe you should slow down," I muttered, quickening my pace.

"You are so funny," Murisha laughed.

I glared at her back.

The path remained narrow, twisting among the trees and periodically crossing streams and gullies. Woody forest smells and flickering sunlight added to the beauty of the day.

By mid-morning the trail started to incline, stressing my calves and deepening my breathing. "Maybe you should be carrying this basket," I hollered. Murisha giggled but didn't slow. When we finally did stop, we stood on a cliff overlooking a six-metre wide gorge that dropped at least fifteen metres to swirling water. I stayed well back from the edge.

"How do we ...?"

Murisha just tilted her head and pointed. Now, I'm not the best at guessing distance, but about one hundred metres in front and another twenty metres above us, was a narrow vine bridge crossing the ravine.

"It is very strong," Murisha reassured.

I said nothing, but my legs tightened and my mouth felt dry. By the time we reached the bridge my heart was pounding. Four support vines were tied to trees on either ledge. The sides and floor of the bridge, woven from thick vines, reminded me of fish netting.

"No," I said. "You can't be serious."

Murisha ignored me, scampering across gracefully. Reaching the other side she turned to encourage me. "Come on, Kiara, we have to hurry!"

Now, I'm not *really* afraid of heights, but this was daunting. We were high above the rushing waters and sharp rocks stared up at me. Cautiously, I edged onto the bridge, grasping the sides tightly. Each time I moved one foot, the netting shifted under the other, and the whole bridge would sway.

"I don't like this," I complained while taking another step.

"Kiara, hurry!" Murisha shouted her focus on something behind me. When she reached for her bow, I knew it was serious. Fighting nausea and sudden dizziness I moved a few steps forward, still desperately grasping those upper vines. A loud snarling from behind, made crossing the bridge seem suddenly easier. Fear unleashed hidden strength and I practically ran to Murisha, not even holding on the remaining distance. She grabbed my arm and pointed. A beautiful black panther was testing the bridge with its front paw, snarling in frustration.

Murisha shot a warning arrow to one side of the big cat, close enough to cause it to jump back. It growled angrily, glaring at us with wild eyes before heading back into the trees.

"You said we were protected!" I accused angrily, my legs shaking.

"Only if you stay close," she retorted putting her bow back over her shoulder. "Now you believe."

I nodded.

"You *must* shadow me!" she said, her eyes blazing. "The jungle can be very dangerous if you are not protected!"

Swallowing a saucy reply I sat on the ground for a rest. Murisha passed me a water skin from the pack I carried.

"Is it much further?" I managed to ask between gulps.

"No," Murisha shook her head. "We will be at the Sacred Site soon. Just one more bridge to cross, and then a set of stone stairs to climb."

"Okay," I sighed. "Almost there."

From that point on I truly did shadow Murisha, never falling more than one or two paces behind. I wasn't getting beyond that circle of protection again, if I could help it. The second bridge, made of the same vines as the first, stretched over a dry canyon, ten or fifteen metres across. This time I scampered across first, not looking down. Murisha laughed at me, knowing fear, not bravery pushed my feet.

Our path leveled as we neared the true volcanic base. Trees thinned giving way to a short flatland. The wind, cool off the ocean, created swaying patterns in the tall grasses.

"Just the stairs now," Murisha said.

A winding stairway, seemingly carved in the stone, climbed the mountain wall. It arched upward to our right following the volcano's silhouette.

"You will see a flat clearing in the volcanic cone at the top," Murisha stated as she reached the first step. "We will stop there to prepare for your meeting."

"*My* meeting!" I sputtered, staying close. "What about you?"

"I will ready things for you," she replied, "but it is you who must seek council with the Great One at the Seeing altar."

"Where's that?" I asked, not wanting more surprises.

"Near the smoke at the volcanic edge," she explained, "there is a small stone table that Father uses as an altar when he seeks council."

This was sounding stranger and stranger. "Murisha," I said haltingly, "Did you ever ... talk to ... it?"

"Oh, no," she replied, "but I have watched my father here. The god will only answer those questions of utmost purity and importance."

"How do you know my question merits the god's answer?"

"My father told me so," Murisha answered with complete faith.

Sweat dripped down the back of my neck and my calf muscles were aching. "I hope this is worth it," I mumbled under my breath as we continued to climb. The hot sun and the exertion were beginning to affect my mood.

"After all this, he better be home!" I growled.

Of course, Murisha just laughed.

Nine

What a workout! I counted at least 510 steps, give or take. But I must say, the view from the stairs was amazing, making the climb almost worth it just to see the panorama of colour in all directions. Pausing near the summit, Murisha pointed out the sandy shore of her village, though we were too far off to discern any other details. From this height, it was obvious that Kikila was an island. Turquoise waters stretched in all directions. To the north there *was* another small island … and maybe to the west but haziness masked that direction. No other landmasses were visible, just ocean and distant clouds.

When we finally reached the summit, I flopped to the ground exhausted, my breathing ragged and legs aching. Murisha, on the other hand, still looked as fresh as when we started earlier that morning. She stood over my gasping body oblivious to my distress.

"No time for rest yet, Kiara," she said her eyes twinkling with excitement. I tried not to listen. "Come on big sister," she badgered. "Get up."

Reluctantly I pulled myself to standing and looked around.

"Alright, we're here, Murisha," I said smiling tiredly. "Now what?"

"Well, Kiara, we are now very near the god." Her voice was soft and filled with respect. "We must prepare for your audience."

I looked past her, assessing our surroundings. A flat shelf of about twenty metres surrounded the dark central volcanic pit. Faint wisps of smoke hung over the crevice, suggesting some hidden activity. Directly in front of us, near the edge of the pit was the altar that Murisha had spoken of. It was very simple in construction, consisting of a large polished, flat rectangular stone supported on each side by blocks. It reached to no more than my knee level in height. A smooth flat stone on the ground before the table provided a sitting surface.

The volcanic shelf itself had low bushes and grasses scattered over most of its surface. To our left was a beautiful old tree; unlike any I'd seen before, either on the island or back home. Its thick gnarly trunk spread open as multiple branches reached upward stretching high into the air. Leaves were long and thin, with beautiful colouration giving an appearance of shivering movement as we watched. Their main colour was dark red with a central silver stripe and faint silver wisps radiating to the edges. Small dark green berries gathered in clusters from many of the branches.

"What is that?" I asked, awed by the tree's beauty.

"That is the Seeing Tree," said Murisha reverently. "It is the only such tree on Kikila. My father believes it one of the most sacred treasures of our island." She paused momentarily to take a drink of water. "Its leaves and fruit are needed in the ritual that you must do."

"It is … majestic!" I said, staring.

Abruptly, Murisha pulled the backpack from my shoulders and began emptying its contents. "Kiara, we must get a move on," she said marking the sun's position.

"Shouldn't we rest for a few minutes?" I asked hopefully.

Murisha wasn't listening. "You make a small fire while I gather some ingredients," she ordered. "There are lots of brush and dried twigs that you can use."

Without even waiting for an answer, she headed toward the Seeing Tree.

"What am I doing here?" I thought for the hundredth time as I gathered the wood and brush. Events were rapidly getting beyond anything I'd imagined. "For Murisha," I reasoned, "I'm doing this for her."

I built a small circle of stones to contain the fire and then carefully constructed my wooden fuel. Using matches from our Cessna's emergency supplies I had a nice little blaze crackling in no time. Just as I finished, Murisha returned with a single, large, silver streaked leaf, and a handful of berries.

"Boil some water," she instructed passing me a copper like pot and the water skin from the backpack.

While I balanced the water filled pot on the edges of some stones over the flickering fire, Murisha was busy with other preparations. First, using a wooden bowl and a long rounded stone, she crushed the berries making a thick green soupy liquid. Next, the shimmering red and silver leaf was shredded and dropped into the now simmering water that I'd prepared.

Murisha reached into her pack once again, retrieving a beautiful multi-coloured shawl. "You must wear this," she explained as she wrapped my head until only my face was exposed. A second similarly coloured cloth was wrapped around my shoulders. When sitting, it covered me completely.

"Is all this necessary?" I asked softly.

"Yes," she replied solemnly, "It is all part of an ancient ritual."

Trying not to spill any of the now, boiling red liquid, she carefully removed it from the flames using two forked twigs.

Putting this on the ground to cool, she passed me the thick, green, soupy stuff in the wooden bowl.

"You alone will drink of this," she said. "This nourishment is provided through the graces of the god of this island, his gift to you."

Tentatively I raised the slurry to my lips, taking a small sip. Surprised by its sweetness, I drank every drop as Murisha voiced encouragement. Though cool to touch, warmth radiated throughout my entire body almost immediately after finishing it.

"This heated drink is to be shared and requires that you give a blood offering to the god," continued Murisha jabbing my index finger with the tip of her dagger. Calmly, I watched a few drops of my blood fall into the leaf tea. That green drink was potent. My nervousness vanished and a sense of peace filled my being.

Swirling the copper pot in circles, Murisha reached up toward the sky murmuring soft rhythmic words. She transferred the tea mixture to me, cradling my hands in hers around the warm vessel. Responding to upward pressure from Murisha's hands, I wordlessly stood and followed her to the altar where she, and then I, bowed deeply. I placed the copper pot on the altar and sat on the flat stone in a crossed leg lotus position. Somehow, I knew to do this. Time slowed; my movements seemed to take forever. I could feel the wind on my bare face like never before. Noises around me became easier to hear and colours seemed more vibrant. Murisha whispered calming words to me and chanted some singsong verses I couldn't decipher. She mimed sipping from her fingers to remind me to drink from the pot and then motioned for me to throw the remainder of the drink into the pit before us. As I completed her directions, sparks rose from the pit and a black smoke flowed toward me. Murisha smoothly backed away from the altar.

I could feel faint tremors in the ground — in the very air around me. Smoke surrounded me, thin tendrils licking at my folded legs. Yet, I felt no fear. Murisha's chanting in the background helped calm me. The smoke swirled, enveloping me much like a glove covering a hand, and I was in darkness. My eyes burned slightly and my nose itched, but there was no smoke smell. Weird!

My skin started to tingle and I heard a faint buzzing in my ears. A light breeze seemed to flow through me, chilling my exposed face. I became increasingly aware of my breathing, noticing the muscles used to breathe in and the warmth of the air I exhaled. I could hear my pulse and had trouble swallowing. Colourful patterns of lights surrounded me with beauty and calmness. Every sense seemed awake — alert.

It's hard to describe everything that happened after that. Images flowed into my mind and peaceful warmth filled me. I could see the volcano, the island of Kikila, the sea and surrounding islands from above. At the edges of this vision, were thick dark clouds, sealing this land in and everything else out. I knew that this barrier separated Kikila from our world and many others as well. There was no set or easy route through the clouds and this was the way it was meant to be. Physical or cultural exchanges with the outer worlds could bring damage to both by upsetting the "rules" that controlled each place. Accidents, like what happened to me and my family, were rare and therefore didn't cause much harm. Words formed in my mind, blunt words, but they carried with them a deep feeling — a love.

Kiara, you must not choose to leave the land of Kikila. You have shared the blood ceremony and are forever linked to this land and its people. Accidental mingling of worlds cannot be controlled but the purposeful passage of Kikilian magic beyond the clouds is not allowed. All events cause ripples that can have long lasting effects.

To you, this seems cruel and unfair. And you are right to think this, but, blood has been shared, and you now carry within you, part of the magic. You and your blood sister are forever linked, beyond just language. If you willingly seek to leave this island, you will destroy more than your sisterhood. Indeed, such a choice will cause each of you to suffer and possibly even die.

Ten

"Wake up, Kiara!" It sounded like Murisha, but she seemed far away. Water splashed over my face and a pair of hands gently cradled my cheeks. "It is over my sister," she said softly. "Wake up!"

Though sitting in bright sunlight, I was still seeing fog and my eyes refused to focus. Visions swirled inside my mind competing for attention. Emotions, ancient and fleeting coursed through me. I knew — I *knew* from the ache in my heart that they were real. Tears streamed down my cheeks and my body shook with sobs. Murisha held me, patiently waiting for the shadow to pass.

Wearily, I straightened my legs and arched my back, stretching. Sniffling, I dried my tears with the shawl, comforted by Murisha's quiet presence. When I finally trusted myself to talk, I turned to my blood sister and took her hand.

"Murisha, if I choose to leave Kikila with my family, it will break the blood bond that we have."

Murisha nodded, but said nothing.

"It would, or could possibly … kill one or both of us," I continued my voice shaking slightly. "The Mountain god told me this."

Murisha stared at me like a wise old woman, smiling slightly. "The blood bond is a very serious thing," she answered. "My father warned me of this." She placed two fingers on her lips and then touched my forehead.

"Whatever happens, Kiara, I am glad of this time. You have brightened my life."

We sat there, side-by-side, holding hands for many minutes, sharing a peaceful communion of sorts. It didn't, or rather couldn't last as reality beckoned. Blowing wind and swirling dust broke the spell, startling us back to our surroundings. Strange yet beautiful colours were gathering on the horizon.

"A storm will be here tonight, or by morning," said Murisha, her forehead wrinkled in thought. "My father cautioned me of this. We must hurry to get back to the village."

I don't remember much of that journey back. Scenery seemed to flow by, with me more a spectator than participant, though my legs kept moving. I do know that Murisha and I held hands all the way. We arrived in the village near dusk. I was tired and confused and my heart was heavy. How could I choose? Was there really any choice?

Murisha guided me to my parent's hut and gave me a hug. Still not thinking clearly, I kissed her forehead and then watched her silently move away, tears running down both her cheeks. None of this seemed real. Winds were beginning to swirl and dark ominous clouds filled the sky, mirroring the storm of emotions that was building in me.

Maybe we could just stay here I thought … hoped … as I pushed through the beaded entrance. Inside the hut, my eyes took in the telltale signs in a glance. "Nooo," I moaned. All of the family things we had unpacked were missing. Our straw beds no longer had blankets, and Dad and Aiden weren't anywhere to be seen.

Mom, sitting at the table to my left must have seen me enter. "Kiara, thank God you're back!" she said jumping up. My eyes widened when I saw she was wearing a flight suit.

"I can't go Mom!" I shouted. "I have to stay here or Murisha will die!"

"Honey, sit down," she replied in a soothing voice. "Tell me why you think that."

I let her lead me to a bamboo bench by the back wall. Words tumbled out, tangled with emotion and tears. "The Mountain god said if I choose to leave Kikila, Murisha could be hurt and me too. The blood bond will be broken ... she might die ... I might die!" Sobs erupted once again. "Stay here with me, Mom," I pleaded. "Don't leave!"

As I babbled, my mother poured me a glass of water and dropped four or five little pills into the liquid. She swirled it around dissolving the medicine. "This will relax you a bit, Kiara," she said passing it to me. "Now try and stop your crying, honey. Everything will be okay." She put her arm around me as I drank. "We know how much you love Murisha and we know you'd never choose to leave if it could cause either of you harm."

Dad and Aiden arrived outside the tent, I heard their voices approaching.

"Aiden, are you sure there's nothing in the plane from this island?" my father asked. "The Shaman was very particular that nothing be taken. He seemed to think it could somehow affect our flight."

"Yes, Dad, I'm sure," he answered. "I checked everything ... twice! You have to remember to leave your walking stick."

When they came through the door, the first thing I noticed was their flight suits — all clean and stain free. The second was

Blueberries and Coal & Inside the Triangle   167

Aidan's hair. It was cut short, like he wore it in Greenwood.

"No," I shouted. "I don't want to go!"

I tried to stand but my muscles were wobbly and I slumped back against my mother.

Relief registered in Dad's face when he saw me. "Kiara! Thank God you're here. I thought we might have to go looking for you."

I tried to answer but my tongue felt thick and my eyes were going blurry. "I, I, I'mmm n ... n ... noott, not g ... g ... goooinng," I stammered, tears dripping off my cheeks.

My mom put her finger to her lips. "Harvey, please be quiet," she said. "Kiara has had a very stressful day and she needs to rest." She helped me lie on the one of the straw mattresses. In a quiet voice, she continued, "It's pretty much what Sitkeem told us. Kiara cannot choose to leave without breaking some of the island taboos."

"So, she's decided she can't hurt Murisha?"

"Yes, her choice is to stay."

I smiled, relieved that my parents understood and then promptly conked out.

Eleven

Mmmmmmmmmmm — a loud low humming filled the air. "Where am I?" I mumbled, my speech thick with sleep. Opening my eyes, I found that my head was on Aiden's shoulder and we were in the backseat of the Cessna!

"You fell asleep," he answered.

Struggling to sit up I realized that my wrap dress had been replaced by my flight suit and I now wore my boots and Mae West, as well. My helmet was under my seat. Confused, I shook my head and blinked my eyes, trying to figure out where we were and what was happening. A feeling of déjà vu filled me.

"Kikila … Murisha …."

"You sure were sound asleep," Aiden commented, showing no understanding of my mutterings.

I turned my gaze to the front seat where Dad was reaching for the radio mike.

"Miami control," he said, "This is flight 471. Can you read us?"

"Roger 471, we read you. We lost you there for a bit. Not a great day to be flying, the weather is deteriorating. Winds are gusting and visibility is dropping."

As if in response to the ATC's words, the plane unexpectedly lurched down and to the right from a sudden forceful gust of wind. From the back seat, I saw Dad fight with the controls to steady the plane. "Get your helmets on," he ordered through clenched teeth. "And make sure your life vest is secure. This wind is really picking up."

"Miami control, we are over water, approaching the coast. Fuel is low and the winds *are* high. We may need to put down on the shore!"

"Keep us informed, 471, and we'll send rescue support."

Dad struggled to straighten the plane after another powerful gust shook the craft. The efforts of flying the plane made it impossible for him to get his helmet on. Each time he let go of the controls with one of his hands, the plane bucked, dipped or veered to one side or another. "Dad, put on your helmet!" I shouted, trying to fight the confusion my mind felt.

He ignored my advice. "Just hold on tight, everybody. I'll lower our altitude to get a visual on where we are." The plane dipped, and the descent was very rough. The altimeter dropped from 4000 metres to below 1800 metres without any change in the outside surroundings.

"Harvey," shouted Mom, "look in front there — an opening in the clouds."

The right wing dipped despite Dad's efforts and the plane began to dive and spin. Mom, Aiden and I screamed frantically. Dad manoeuvred various foot controls and pulled up on the steering yoke to steady the plane. Then suddenly, the spin was over. Dad pulled up the nose of the plane and jubilantly looked over at Mom. He laughed wildly and gave a shout of triumph!

Aiden hooted his appreciation. Me, I felt like somebody kicked me in the ribs. My memories came roaring back. "Murisha!" I screamed at the front seats. "You made me leave!"

Mom turned around and looked at me, obviously puzzled. "What are you talking about?"

"Nooo," I moaned, worried for my friend.

"Will you be quiet?" Aiden hollered, elbowing me in the side. "Get a grip!"

"Harvey, I see land," Mom shouted. "Out my window, there's the shore!"

"We're going to make it, Janet," he answered. "We can land on that long, flat, empty section of the beach shore." In a lower voice he added, "We don't have enough fuel to go much further." Into his mike, "Miami control, this is flight 471. I'm going to land on the shore of this coast. No fuel to go further."

"Roger, 471, we have you on radar. You are about twenty miles or ... just under thirty kilometres southwest of us. Rescue vehicles are being dispatched."

"Oh my, God," I thought. "We did this before."

The Cessna circled the sandy area, gradually losing altitude and air speed. "Okay, everybody, hold on tight," Dad said, as he angled the plane down. "Because of the sand, I'll almost have to stall it when we touch down so there'll be very little taxiing."

My mind was still groggy from whatever drug Mom had given me, but I knew what was happening. "Dad, put on your helmet," I screamed.

Too late.

On contact with the beach our front wheel collapsed, immediately jamming the nose of our plane into the ground. We came to an abrupt halt and Dad, without a helmet, crashed headfirst into the dash of the control panel. Mom also hit the dash, but her helmet took some of the force as did her right arm when she tried to brace herself.

Aiden and I were thrown forward against the back of the front seats but were injury free ... just like in Kikila!

I'm afraid this second time around, I wasn't as 'together' as I was in Kikila. When the firemen pulled me and Aiden from the plane, I was screaming and crying. I think it was those drugs.

Blueberries and Coal & Inside the Triangle

Then, as we were directed to ambulances, I began barking out orders to the Emergency Medical Technicians. "You there, be careful! My dad's got a fractured skull and my mom broke her nose," I shouted. "And his right leg is broke," I pointed, "and so is her left arm. They need splints!"

One of the techs kept telling me to slow my breathing and calm down.

The next few hours were a blur. Ambulances took us to some Miami hospital. My father ... you guessed it ... did indeed have a broken leg and a fractured skull. He was taken to the operating room for trephination because of a blood clot. My mom had the same broken arm as in Kikila, a mild concussion and, yes, a broken nose.

I knew they'd be fine. After all, this was just a rerun of our first crash. The staff at the hospital, however, thought my lack of concern a bit odd. It's a stress response they kept saying.

When I tried to tell them about the previous crash and Kikila, all I got was queer looks. It didn't help that Aiden remembered nothing.

"What do you mean you don't remember any Kikila?" I shouted at him in the Emergency Room.

"Kiara, I don't know what you're talking about," Aiden replied looking at me with the same look as everybody else. "Maybe you hit your head or something."

Apparently the medical people agreed. I ended up having some head x-rays and a special CAT scan of my brain during the three days that we stayed in Miami's finest. The tests were normal of course, so next in, came the mental health team. They said my story was made up; a fantasy created as a result of fear and stress from the crash. Similar to post traumatic stress disorder, a stuffy old guy with a goatee kept saying. "She may need counseling ...."

By the time we flew back to Nova Scotia, courtesy of the Canadian Armed Forces, I learned not to discuss Murisha and Kikila with anyone. I knew it was true, but if I kept talking about it, they'd think I was crazy.

On a positive note, Mom and Dad are mending quite well from their injuries, just like I knew they would. And Aiden is fine, already looking forward to seeing his friends in Greenwood again. Me, well, I feel sad and I miss my little sister.

Sigh.

I know *why* nobody believes me! But that doesn't help, because it's not me with the problem!

Sniff.

My brother and my parents don't remember and they were with me, so of course, everyone thinks *my* memory must be screwy. Well, news people, I'm the only one that *can* remember! Time got twisted inside that triangle. Maybe only an hour passed here, but I know we were there, in Kikila, for almost six full months!

Like, how else would I know about trephination, medicinal herbs, dyes and tropical native diets? It was real all right ... something happened to *their* memories not mine!

It makes me so mad ... and ... sad.

Sniff.

Maybe, because I didn't want to leave and was asleep during the takeoff, my memory wasn't wiped clean, like theirs. I don't know ... maybe I'll never know. But I'm betting since I left without choosing to — and *I'm* still healthy, that Murisha is fine too!

I sure hope so, anyway.

If something did happen to her, I should be able to feel it, don't you think? I mean, we are blood sisters.

Sigh.

So here I sit, writing in my diary, making sure I'll always remember what really happened. I only have to touch the

Blueberries and Coal & Inside the Triangle   **173**

snakebite scars on my leg to know how real it all was. And it's so easy to remember Murisha's smile and her voice.

The island, the people, the games, exploring … at least I have those memories. The tiny people of Kikila looked so fierce, yet were kind and helpful. Different is just that, not worse, not better. I never want to forget all that I saw and what I learned.

I left my best friend behind. Aiden had friends, Mom and Dad met people. How can that be wiped out? The Mountain god was right; it's NOT fair!

Sniff.

No more tears! I'm going back someday … at least I'm going to try … I have to try. Maybe I can convince Mom and Dad to do this trip again after they recover — if Mom will ever fly again. I mean, to them, they didn't get to do their planned vacation — and they don't remember the Bermuda Triangle issues. Yeah, that's what I'll do. They have to listen.

And I'll remind them of some things to make them curious — things I know they are already starting to question. Our tans for one. How did we all get so brown if we didn't spend time outside in the sun? And the first aid kit, it's half-empty of antiseptic and gauze from treating Dad's injuries. Then, there are the missing sleeping pills, the mismatched Cessna propeller and front strut. And what about our hair? Mine is a good fifteen centimetres longer than when we left … so is Mom's. Aiden's is lighter but he and Dad got crew cuts in Kikila just before we left.

By the time I finish 'reminding' them, they'll all want to find their lost memories.

Me, I just want to see my friend.

Wait for me, Murisha. I'm coming back, if not this year, then next year, or later when I'm old enough to get my own pilot's license. I'll never forget you, little sister. I hope *you* can remember me.

I love you.
Sniff.

CPSIA information can be obtained at www.ICGtesting.com
Printed in the USA
LVOW13s0340051113

359968LV00001B/19/P

9 781460 223918